What Pooh Might Have Said To Dante
and other futile speculations

What Pooh Might Have Said To Dante
and other futile speculations

Manny Rayner

Copyright © Manny Rayner, 2012
ISBN: 978-1-105-52071-6

Contents

Foreword viii
Acknowledgements ix
With apologies to Ambrose Bierce x

I Children   1

Alice's Adventures in Wonderland 3
Disney's The Little Mermaid 5
The Railway Children meet Atlas Shrugged 7
Harry Potter 10
The Stinky Cheese Man 14
The Enchanted Castle 15
The Faraway Tree Stories 18
Help! Mom! There Are Liberals Under My Bed! . . 20
Kalas, Alfons Åberg 21
Max est fou de jeux vidéo 24

II Trash   27

Fear of Flying 29

Les liaisons dangereuses	32
Megan's Mark	34
Heretics of Dune	36
Hoki: A Manny Rayner novel based on Shibumi	38
Sarah	41
Skye O'Malley	43
Devil of the Highlands	44
Jemima Puddleduck meets a French trash novel	45
Breaking Dawn	47

III Literachuh   53

En attendant Godot	55
1984 meets Lolita	57
À la recherche du temps perdu	60
Paradise Lost	61
The Crying of Lot 49	65
Good Omens meets Madame Bovary	67
The Picture of Dorian Gray	70
The Trial	73
À rebours	77
Mary Poppins meets Pride and Prejudice	79
Pale Fire	82

IV Science Fiction   85

I, Robot meets Twilight	87
L'écume des jours	93

The Hitchhiker's Guide to the Galaxy	94
Time for the Stars	97
Roderick	100
Infinite Jest	105
The Player of Games	116
Cat's Cradle	118
Orbitsville	121
Twin Planets	123
Frankenstein	125

V Miscellaneous fiction 127

The Three Musketeers meet The Lord of the Rings .	129
The History Boys	131
If Le marin de Gibraltar were a woman	134
Sherlock Holmes meets The Little Prince	137
The Godfather	141
Go Ask Alice	143
Scott Pilgrim versus The World	145
253: A Novel	149
Overqualified	152
Vox	154

VI Chess and Other Geekiness 155

Are You A Geek?	157
Revolution in the 70s meets Fahrenheit 451	159
The Integral Trees	162

Finnegans Wake	163
Kasparov v Karpov 1986-1987 meets Black Swan	165
Dude, Where's My Country?	168
Karpov's Caro Kann: Panov's Attack	169
The Flanders Panel	172

VII Science   175

The Selfish Gene	177
Bonk	178
Gravitation	181
QED	183

VIII Linguistics, Philosophy and Sociology   185

Wittgenstein of the Camel Squadron	187
Our Magnificent Bastard Tongue	189
Comment parler des livres que l'on n'a pas lus?	194
Against Method	196
Stuff White People Like	202
Crowds and Power	203
Fate, Time and Language	207
Twilight and Philosophy	211

IX Poetry   213

The Hunting Of The Snark	215
McGonnagal's Collected Poems	216
Archy and Mehitabel	217

Sonnet XVIII (new improved version) 218
Diwan över Fursten av Emgión 219

X Religion   221

Star Maker 223
The 7 Habits of Highly Effective People 225
La tentation de saint Antoine 228
The New Testament 230
The Holy Bible 233
Oppdageren 237
Pooh Bear meets The Divine Comedy 240

Foreword

Sometime around the end of 2008, my friend Jordan sent me an invite to join **goodreads.com**. She said I'd like it. At first I couldn't really see the point of entering all your books on an internet database, writing reviews of them, and comparing them with reviews other people had written ... but, remarkably quickly, I found I had become an addict. I have now posted well over a thousand reviews. This book contains the eighty or so that I like best.

So what *is* the point, you may ask? I'm not quite sure I can explain, but let me try. Your first reaction, if you're a sensible person, is that it's silly: how can you possibly think of something new and interesting to say about *Hamlet*, or *Jane Eyre*, or even *Harry Potter and the Deathly Hallows*? But every person reads the book in their own way and has their own associations; to themselves, to the people they know, to other books they've read. Writing about a book is a way of writing about your whole life, often some aspect of it that you'd forgotten but which the book made you remember. In many of these reviews, what I find myself doing is talking to one of the characters, or having that character talk to a character from a different book.

I don't want to make exaggerated claims for Goodreads. Like all social network sites, it's a tremendous time-waster. People have bitchy conversations and fight for meaningless status rewards (there is intense competition to see who receives most votes for their reviews). They get swept away by pointless fads like putting down Twilight or writing reviews in a particular style. But there's a positive side to it too, and on a good day it can almost feel like a modern equivalent of an 18th century literary salon. I'd like to dedicate this book to all the new friends I've made here over the last few years: BirdBrian, Ian, Mariel, Paul, Moira, Brad, Tatiana, Whitaker, MJ, Ceridwen, the several Davids, Jonathans, Ellens, Tims, Sarahs, Barbaras, Johns, Abigails, Chrisses, Jennifers, Simons, Allans, Matts, Jessicas, Marys, Marks, Erics and Mikes, Aerin, Oriana, mp, Alfonso, Carlo, K.D, Emir, Ryan, Sandybanks, Hayes, Bettie, Tuck, Plch, Kat, Robert, Hazel, Julia, Pavel, Donna, Isaiah, La Pointe, Karen, Kristin, Praj, Trevor, Choupette, Madeline, Joshua, Vinaya, Buck, Kinga, shovelmonkey, Luka, Nick, Matthieu, Bram, Kristen, Marvin, Des, Cassandra, Traveller, Dulac3, SubterraneanCatalyst, aussiescribbler, Vivi, Bri, Josh, Peycho and Ted. And, last but definitely not least, notgettingenough. Not, my life would be dull indeed without you.

Acknowledgements

This book owes its existence to the many people on Goodreads who encouraged me to put it together. Thank you, everyone! More specific thanks are due to notgettingenough, who gave excellent advice on layout and formatting, proof-read the entire manuscript, and generally contributed her expertise as a publisher and editor; Jordan, who co-authored two of the reviews (*Bonk* and *Paradise Lost*); Martha, who designed the front cover; and BirdBrian, Ian, Mariel and Yllacaspia, who read and commented various drafts of the manuscript. Much appreciated in all cases.

Manny Rayner

Geneva, February 2012

With apologies to Ambrose Bierce

goodreads, *n.* Website designed to prevent people who enjoy books from finding time to read them.

review, *v.i.* Demonstrate, through a short essay, appreciation for one's own wit.

Part I

Children

Alice's Adventures in Wonderland
Lewis Carroll

"Good gracious!" said Alice, "I do believe I'm inside a review!" She turned to the Hatter and the March Hare.

"Well, let me see. Here is the title, and here is the date I read it. That must be today. Now I need to explain the plot and the overall point."

"There is no plot," said the March Hare disagreeably.

"And there is no point," agreed the Hatter.

He poured a little hot tea on the Dormouse's nose, making it wake with a start.

"The book breaks new ground," it said rapidly in a high, sing-song voice. "Intentionally eluding easy assignment to any traditional category, it anticipates the twentieth century's fascination with the relationship between the signifier and the signified, and wittily deconstructs the primacy of meaning and the rationality of thought." Then it went back to sleep again, and began to snore gently.

"Whatever did that mean?" asked Alice, surprised.

"Why is a Derrida like a derrière?" replied the Hatter.

"I don't know," said Alice.

"I don't know either," said the Hatter triumphantly.

"It would be *reasonable*", said Alice, in the grown-up tone she had sometimes heard her sister use, "It would be *reasonable* for you to explain what the book is about, so that I could put that in my review."

"It would be *reasonable*," said the Hatter, "to expect hot premarital sex in a Stephenie Meyer novel. But don't imagine you'll find any."

Alice couldn't think of anything to reply to this, so she turned away without another word. When she was almost out of earshot, she thought she heard the Hatter shout something after her that might have been "Foucault!"

Disney's The Little Mermaid
Disney Corporation

This much-loved story by ~~Hans Christian Andersen~~ a team of anonymous Disney screenwriters tells how a beautiful young mermaid falls in love with a human prince. One day, she saves his life when his boat sinks during a storm. The prince wakes up on the shore, but ~~the mermaid has gone, and he never sees her; he only remembers the human girl who finds him shortly afterwards~~ he only sees the mermaid briefly as she escapes back to the water, and does not guess her secret. He in turn falls in love with the girl he believes has rescued him.

The mermaid is consumed by her love for the prince, and in the end adopts the desperate expedient of concluding a pact with the Sea Witch. The mermaid will gain legs and look like a woman. However, she will lose her beautiful voice. ~~Also, every step she takes will feel as through she is walking on sharp knives.~~ The mermaid accepts the offer, and becomes a human. She is taken into the prince's household.

The mermaid's only chance of salvation is to be loved by the prince. ~~Alone, and without her voice, her chances are slim.~~ Luckily, she has her three zany friends to help her: a singing crab, a kind fish and a goofy seabird. Together, they concoct a series of ingenious plans, which nearly succeed in making the prince kiss her and break the spell.

But meanwhile, the prince is planning to marry ~~the girl who found~~ him ~~on the shore after the shipwreck~~, the Sea Witch, who has disguised herself to look like the mermaid and moreover has her stolen voice. ~~The prince is torn, for he does indeed find the mermaid very beautiful, but he feels that the right decision is to marry the girl he incorrectly believes was his rescuer. He takes her as his wife,~~ and the ~~mermaid knows her heart is broken.~~

At the last minute, the mermaid's ~~sisters come to her with a~~

~~knife, and say that she can still save herself by killing the prince and his bride. But she refuses, and chooses death for herself instead.~~ zany friends succeed in unmasking the Sea Witch's imposture. There is a bloody showdown, where the prince and the mermaid kill the Sea Witch. Then the prince marries the mermaid and they live happily ever after.

It is hard not to be swept away by the story's relentlessly ~~bleak~~ upbeat message. Great sacrifices ~~can be utterly in vain~~ are invariably rewarded, and true love ~~may end in the most appalling tragedy~~ always triumphs over adversity.

The Railway Children meet Atlas Shrugged
E. Nesbit and Ayn Rand

It's a capacity crowd tonight at the Surrealist Boxing Stadium, and everyone's wondering if *The Railway Children* have a chance against *Atlas Shrugged*. I can see them in the blue corner, I must say they look nervous, they know they're behind on weight and reach but their supporters are out in force, that's always worth a lot, Bobbie is trying to calm Phyllis, she's whispering something in her ear. And it's the bell, *Atlas Shrugged* goes straight for them, oh no, she's already got the children's father arrested, we could be looking at a first round knockout here, but the mother rallies, she's ducking and weaving and she's managed to get the kids off to Yorkshire, they move into their new home. The ref is calling time, and I see there's a railway going right past their back garden, I think it's a Taggart line, this is more exciting than we dared hope.

Round two, and Peter tries a right jab, he's stealing coal from the Taggart depot, *Atlas Shrugged* comes out swinging again, the Station Master catches him, will Peter be joining his father in prison? the crowd is going crazy! But no, he lets him off with a caution, very weak-willed, an unexpected lack of decisiveness from the favorite, we thought it would be easy but now the match could be anyone's, time again. We can see John Galt talking with *Atlas Shrugged* in the red corner, wonder what he's saying, this will be interesting.

Round three, and *Atlas Shrugged* has a new tactic, the children's mother is ill, high fever, looks very bad for her, she's pressed back against the ropes, this could be it, but these kids have real fighting spirit, they subvert the Old Gentleman's Objectivist principles and he's helping them! I must say this is amazing, he's sent the children a hamper and they're nursing their mother back to health, Bobbie persuades the Doctor to help her too, *Atlas Shrugged* looking very disappointed at that missed opportunity, and now it's time again.

Round four, and *Atlas Shrugged*'s thinking that all that gratuitous help the children have received is going to weaken them, they certainly look defensive, just barely blocking her attacks, but suddenly they're counter-attacking, they've helped a Russian refugee, repaying their debt to society and delivering a solid left to *Atlas Shrugged*'s midriff, she's winded, Dagny has dropped her bracelet and Peter's kicked it out of the ring, for the first time the kids have the initiative and the crowd is loving every minute, I can feel the tide turning here, and this time *Atlas Shrugged* is glad to hear the bell.

Round five, and *Atlas Shrugged* is very cautious, she can feel the kids are going to try something, what is it, yes! Jim Taggart's inadequate engineering work has caught up with him, a landslide's blocked the line, Dagny will kill him when she finds out, the kids are landing a hail of blows but can they finish him off, the girls take off their red petticoats and they've turned them into flags, this is pure poetry, I've never seen *Atlas Shrugged* look so sick, they've saved the train and Jim Taggart has to thank them in public! time again and none too early.

Round six, the kids are looking confident, they're pressing *Atlas Shrugged*, she has to try something, oh, this is clever, Perks has a birthday and the kids are collecting presents for him, but I think it's a trap, they've overreached, oh my God, they've definitely gone too far, Perks is calling it charity, he's furious, they underestimated his belief in Objectivism, suddenly *Atlas Shrugged* is landing blow after blow, Phyllis's shoelace has come undone, it's all turned round inside a few seconds, they had victory in sight and now they're fighting for their lives, Bobbie is crying, have they blown it, but no! Perks is weakening, his wife has convinced him the kids meant well, he's shaking their hands, *Atlas Shrugged* can't believe it, a golden chance and once more she failed to take advantage, time!

Round seven, and *Atlas Shrugged* looks like she's already given up, she's barely trying any more, her morale's gone, Hank's having a drink with Wesley Mouch, Robert Stadler's got his hand up Dagny's skirt, the kids land a left hook to the solar plexus followed by a straight right to the jaw, *Atlas Shrugged*'s on the canvas, the ref's started counting, one, two, the kids' father's been acquitted of all charges and released, five, six, Bobby runs towards him shouting Daddy! nine, ten, it's over, Francisco shoots himself, the crowd's on its feet, complete victory for left-wing liberal values, they're carrying the new champions in triumph from the ring, it's a turning point in surrealist boxing history, signing off now.

Harry Potter
J.K. Rowling

I got into an argument the other day with an articulate 17 year old Harry Potter fan — let's call him D — who wanted to know why I was being so nasty in my review of *Deathly Hallows*. What was wrong with it? I offered various structural criticisms: the ending is abrupt and unconvincing, the subplot with the Horcruxes has not been adequately foreshadowed in the earlier volumes, and the book as a whole is overlong and boring. D expressed surprise that I could call *Deathly Hallows* boring, when I'd given five stars to *Madame Bovary* and *Animal Farm*, both of which he considered far duller. The discussion continued for some time. In the end, I said I would write a review summarising my objections to the series as a whole. Here it is.

As I said to D, it's not the books or the author. The early Potter books are cute and entertaining, and J.K. Rowling seems like a nice person — if someone's going to scoop the literary Powerball jackpot, why not her? What I very strongly object to is the way the books have been marketed. About 10 years ago, it seems to me, some clever people figured out a new marketing strategy, which they first applied to Potter; when that came to an end, the same methods were used for Twilight. Both series have enjoyed a level of success which is utterly disproportionate to their quality, and which is also unprecedented in literary history. Twilight clearly follows Potter; I've had several discussions about what preceded Potter, and the answer, everyone seems to agree, is that there was no earlier success story of this kind. Before Potter, there was no YA series of dubious merit that absolutely everyone read.

I think it's uncontroversial that Potter, in terms of literary quality, is better than Twilight, but Twilight has been even more successful. At one point, the four volumes occupied the top four spots in the New York Times bestseller list. On Goodreads, nearly half of the top 50 reviews are of Twilight books. This is an absurd and unnatural state of affairs. Even though Twilight may not be quite as bad as is sometimes made out — I'm one of many people who have tried to defend it — there's no way it deserves this level of attention.

So why is everyone reading it, and why, before that, was everyone reading Potter? As I said, I think it's primarily about the marketing, though I wish I was more sure about the details. Here, at any rate, are some thoughts. First, the publishers are aggressively using economies of scale and deals with third parties. They print very large numbers of copies, and they work together with movie studios, game companies and merchandisers to cross-promote them. I think it's particularly important that a large proportion of the books are sold, not at bookstores, but at normal supermarkets. It's well known that the cover price is usually marked down to the point where the supermarket is not in fact making any profit; they have discovered that they can successfully treat it as a loss leader. This is causing great pain to independent bookstores. Some of them, I have read, have adopted the desperate expedient of buying copies at supermarkets and then reselling them.

Second, let's look at the content and style. Even though Potter and Twilight are fairly different in some ways, they also have many strong similarities. Above all, they are extremely easy to read, at every level. The vocabulary is unchallenging; the sentences are short and simple; most characters are one-dimensional stereotypes; the story is uncomplicatedly plot-driven; there are few references to other works of literature. You can read these books if you're tired, if you're sleepy, if you have poor reading skills, if you've never read anything else. They consequently have a very large potential audience.

Third, they describe a comforting, emasculated world in which most of the things that make our own world so difficult and unpleasant have been removed. Most strikingly, there is no sex; in Harry Potter, which is supposed to be about fairly normal teens, no one masturbates, no girls get pregnant, none of them are labelled sluts because they've had sex with more than one boy (sometimes one is enough, for that matter), no one gets their heart broken and drops out of school or starts taking drugs as a result, no one is stuck in a dead-end relationship that they wish they could escape from, but can't. The worst thing that happens in either series is the sequence in *New Moon* where Edward temporarily leaves Bella. Meyer notoriously doesn't describe Bella's feelings at all, but just leaves several pages blank. Once, in fact not so long ago, most adults would have been embarrassed to be seen reading YA literature of this kind; to start with, the comforting word "YA" hadn't been invented yet, and they would have been reading children's books. Somehow, there's been a shift in standards. You look around you on a bus to see what people are reading, and you can be pretty sure you'll see at least a couple of people over 20 engrossed in Potter or Twilight. It's odd that this has happened, and I wish I understood why.

In conclusion, I couldn't help being struck by the two books D chose to contrast against Potter. D, *Madame Bovary* is going to outlast both of these authors because Emma is a real person who experiences the crazy and contradictory emotions that real people experience when they are very unhappy, and as a result she behaves in a crazy and contradictory way; also, Flaubert, unlike Rowling and Meyer, took a great deal of trouble over his prose, and created some of the most beautiful and ironic passages in world literature. There aren't many books I'd call masterpieces, but this is one of them. And finally, *Animal Farm* is indeed an allegory of the Russian Revolution. More importantly, though, it's about how smart, unscrupulous people manipulate trusting, weak people. Tens of millions of people are reading Potter and Twilight, not because the books are well-written or interesting, but because the readers have been manipulated into buying them by the Napoleons and Squealers of this world. That's what I'm objecting to. Think about it for a moment.

The Stinky Cheese Man
Jon Scieszka

They keep making postmodernism accessible to younger and younger age groups. This is a typical postmodern take on the fairy-story genre — they even present Jack the Giant-Killer as an infinite regress of meta-stories — but it's done skillfully enough that I've met bright 6-year-olds who found it funny and got the point.

Given the inexorable forward march of literary technology, I think that we should have postmodernism for infants available not later than 2035. I can already see a knowing, rather bored-looking baby, wearing a fashionably retro diaper, "putting the book into his mouth" and ironically chewing it. If only I knew how to arrange this, I'm sure I could make some money.

The Enchanted Castle
E. Nesbit

This is a novel I like a lot, which I've experienced in different ways at different points in my life. I first read it when I was six or seven, and thought it was a great story. There are these kids, and they find a castle and a magic ring. At first they think it's an invisibility ring. Then, to their surprise, they find it can make inanimate objects come to life, or make you rich. After a while, they come to a truly startling conclusion: the ring can do *anything at all!* When its latest power wears off, the owner can just tell it what new power it is to acquire. They come up with some creative ideas, which are a lot of fun; one of the best ones is where they find that the statues in the castle's grounds come to life at night, and they can themselves become living statues. One of the statues is a life-size brontosaurus. Like many seven year olds, I loved dinosaurs. This ring was amazing!

But, for some reason, they finally decide that they have to say goodbye to all the magic; the castle ends up as a plain castle, and the statues as plain statues. There was something about a grave, and I could tell it was sad. But the good part was that their nice French governess marries the man whose castle it is, and the children can always go back and visit them. I didn't understand the ending. Why did they have to destroy the magic? That was disappointing. But I loved the rest of it, and books often didn't make sense all the way through. I guessed I would figure it when I was older.

The next time I came back to it, I was eleven or twelve. I'd read *The Lord of the Rings*, and found some interesting parallels. (By the way, I've since checked; no one appears to know if this is coincidence or not). For whatever reason, it isn't clear that the ring is all good. Somehow, when you have it on, no one cares about you. The children notice this, and it rather creeps them out. And there's a love story! I hadn't properly noticed that before. The lord of the castle is quite poor; he's lost his money, and he's going to have to sell his ancestral home. But what makes him most unhappy is that he's also lost his true love. He's pining for her, and doesn't know how to find her again. One day, they're out on a picnic, and the kids tell him that they have a wishing ring. He just has to wish for whatever he most wants, and he'll get it. He figures he'll humor them; he takes the ring, and says "I wish my friend was here". And, at that very moment, the beautiful French governess appears; she was supposed to join them all along, but she's late. It's his true love! This was a cute scene, and I liked the irony too: the adults assume it has to be a miraculous coincidence, but they aren't sure.

I understood the ending better. They give the ring to the castle's lord (he is the rightful owner), but he can't handle it. It makes him feel terrible, and his sanity is at risk. Finally, he makes a decision. His last request will be that the ring become an ordinary wedding ring, and lose all its magic. He'll marry his true love, and keep his castle, but life will just be normal again. This was at any rate satisfyingly romantic. But I still didn't quite get the bit about the statue of Psyche. I had trouble figuring out how you pronounced her name, or who she was. One of the last things that happens, after the magic has gone, is that they find a stone in a secret place, deep in the castle. It's her grave. This was definitely very sad, but why?

I still wouldn't be prepared to say I'm sure I know what this book is about. I believe there's more than one possible interpretation. My 50 year old self, though, thinks it's about what happens when you grow up. When you are a child, you realize, if you are lucky at any rate, that you can potentially use your mind to do anything at all. You can use it to become rich, or conjure life into inanimate objects, or talk with the statues of gods and the illustrious dead. But, in fact, most people choose, of their own free will, not to do any of those things. They bury Psyche, their godlike intelligence, and they get married and have children of their own. And that's both sad and happy.

I admire E. Nesbit for being able to put all this stuff into a book that a seven year old could enjoy. She must have been a remarkable person. Looking at the entry in Wikipedia, I see that she got married when she was only 22, because she had to, and things were complicated and sometimes very painful. *Castle* was published in 1907, when she was 39. I would love to know what she was thinking when she wrote it.

The Faraway Tree Stories
Enid Blyton

I never much liked Enid Blyton when I was a kid, but this one got read out to us aloud sometime in second grade so I had no choice. I don't remember very much of it (I fear I may not really have been paying attention), but there is one incident that stuck in my memory. The kids have found this magical ice-cream vendor who can give you absolutely any flavour you want. All but one of them do the sensible thing and just request their favourite kind. But the smart-ass in the group decides to test the limits of the system, and asks for a sardine ice-cream. And, sure enough, he gets it, and very unpleasant it is too. I can still clearly see the picture of the discomfited-looking child holding the cone, with a fish's tail poking out of the scoop of ice-cream. No doubt the episode resonated with me because I'm also a smart-ass.

I remembered this story the other day when we went out for dinner at the little Tokyo restaurant around the corner from the hotel. I had been diligently practising my restaurant Japanese, and insisted on showing that I could order a beer, say that we wanted five skewers of yakitori, and ask whether they had tempura. But my dinner companion, whom I'll call C to spare her blushes, told me that none of that was necessary. "You just point to things at random in the menu!" she said confidently. "It's all delicious. Let them surprise you."

I wasn't too sure about this, but I let myself be talked into it. Holding the menu so that I couldn't even see it, she called the waitress over and pointed to two items. The waitress turned to me and said something in Japanese that I didn't understand, but judging from her tone of voice it certainly sounded like "Are you sure you want THAT?" Foolishly loyal to my friend, I insisted that we absolutely did, *kudasai*!

After ten minutes, the first of the two items arrived — it was a rather fine type of fried baby octopus, which I loved. I was about to admit that C was right when the waitress brought us the second order.

Well. I said afterwards that it was the most disgusting thing I'd had all year, while C, generous in defeat, said it was the most disgusting thing she'd ever tasted. The dish, whose name I still don't know, consisted of eight little slices of half-centimetre thick, partially thawed, deep-frozen raw beef. You got some soy sauce to dip it in, and that was it. C ate one mouthful and couldn't continue, but, for reasons I still can't explain, I finished the whole lot. Maybe I wanted to show the waitress that I really did know what I was doing, though I doubt she was fooled.

You can understand why I thought of the scene from *The Faraway Tree*. I had stomache-ache all night, but it was nice to know that I wasn't the only smart-ass in the world.

Help! Mom! There Are Liberals Under My Bed!

Katherine DeBrecht

Hey kids! Here's a fun experiment you can do over the holidays. All you need is a copy of this book, some paper, some glue, and a bit of time.

First, pick up the book and look through a few pages. You'll see the words "liberal" and "liberals" in many places. Now, every time you see one of those words, take a little piece of paper, write "Jew" or "Jews" instead, and stick it in on top of the original word! You may make a mess of the first one or two, but you'll soon get the hang of it.

When you've finished, go and read it aloud to a few grown-ups. You'll find their reactions very interesting! Keep a little notebook so that you can remember what they said. If you know anyone old enough to have fought in World War II, that can be particularly educational. But if you can't, people who are Jewish themselves, or have Jewish relatives, are in some ways even better.

Happy experimenting, junior sociologists!

Kalas, Alfons Åberg
Gunilla Bergström

Some subjects are so frightening that there is a de facto taboo on mentioning them at all. I understand, for example, that before Ibsen tackled the subject of hereditary syphilis in *Ghosts*, people refused even to talk about it, and the play prompted an outcry. In this book, Gunilla Bergström bravely describes what a small child's birthday party is *really* like. There is a myth, possibly created by excessive use of rose-tinted spectacles, that they are cute and fun occasions. Any parent who has organized one will know that this is a lie of Orwellian proportions. They are soul-destroying events that are, in most cases, survivable. And, of course, they are socially essential. It's hard to be much more positive than that.

As usual with the early Alfons books, the story is expertly told on two levels. It's Alfons's birthday, and he's going to have a party. Aunt Fifi has come to help out. We're told that "she has no kids of her own, so she is always extra nice to Alfons". The child reader mainly wants to get to the action, but the adult is intrigued by Fifi, who seems to have a rather tragic back-story. She's got a lot of psychological baggage, and is busily trying to use Alfons to help her unpack some it.

Fifi asks how many people Alfons wants to invite. "Just Victor and Milla and me, of course!" says Alfons. All he wants to do is hang out with his gang and get better food. But Fifi is having none of it. She wants a really BIG birthday party, with LOTS of kids. First, she plans to invite the whole street, but Dad steps in and vetoes this. In the end, they compromise on a dozen guests. Fifi goes completely overboard on preparations, which take all week. She's an anal, controlling type who wants to organize everything down to the last detail. (The adult begins to gain some insight into her tragic back-story). She bakes several cakes, which really smell pretty good. Alfons would love to try one, but of course he has to wait until Saturday.

Finally, it's Party Day. All the kids turn up, wearing their best clothes and looking rather shy. But as soon as the cakes come out, everyone relaxes considerably. They agree that Fifi bakes a mean cake, and get progressively higher on sugar. Fifi has a whole activity program mapped out, but the kids respond with less and less enthusiasm and start quarreling. There is a near-crisis when Martin finds that his party bag contains a green lollipop, while his neighbor has a red one. "There is JUST AS MUCH in all the bags!" says Fifi, trying to calm things down. "But it's not the SAME!" growls Martin, who clearly feels he's been short-changed.

Things get more and more out of control, and Fifi can no longer keep the lid on the children's frayed tempers. (The adult reader keeps wondering where Dad is. He's left her to run the whole show). When they get to "Hide and Seek", the kids have had enough of being managed. The girls all go and lock themselves in the bathroom and refuse to play. When they come out, everything degenerates into open warfare. I have read the book several times to 4 year old Samuel, and he loves this picture, which we go over carefully together. "He's pulling her hair ... he's snatched her hot-dog ... she's crying because her balloon has burst ... he's blowing Coke on her dress through the straw ... he tried to grab his party-bag and they're going to fight over it." Samuel is an early fan of extreme realism.

Alfons thinks it's almost a good thing when everyone goes home at 6 pm. Fifi, wearing a fixed smile and clearly on the verge of tears, cleans up and takes out the enormous quantities of uneaten cake to the kitchen. The adult reader feels sorry for her, but at the same time can see that this is the story of her life and that she isn't really very surprised.

But ... there's a happy ending! The next day, Fifi asks Alfons if he liked his birthday party. "Oh yes!" says Alfons. "The cakes were YUMMY! What a good thing you made so many! 'Cause now there's enough ... for my OWN party!" And indeed, Alfons's two best friends have come around as usual, and they're sitting under the table with Alfon's toy animals eating the left-over cake. Alfons is a really nice kid at heart. You can see why Fifi likes him so much.

Max est fou de jeux vidéo
Dominique de Saint-Mars

There's this memorable scene in *Trainspotting* where Ewan McGregor tells you why he does heroin. "Take the best orgasm you've ever had," he explains. "Multiply it by a thousand. And then imagine it going on for two hours. Well, it's like that. We're not *stupid* you know." This book is similar, though aimed at a younger audience; like *Trainspotting* and *Infinite Jest*, it adopts the strategy of showing you both why the activity is so destructive and also why it's so enticing.

Max is about six and has become hooked on video games. At home, he does nothing but sit in front of the screen, controller in hand. His social circle no longer contains anyone except fellow game junkies. When he's forced to leave the house on his own, he takes his GameBoy with him and plays while walking. The cover illustration shows how insanely dangerous this is.

If the book only presented the negative side of the story, it would be worthy but dull. It rises to greatness by also showing the other side, and I was vividly reminded of an incident that occurred when my younger son was about Max's age and also into video games. My Belgian colleague P was visiting, and David wanted to show her how to play *Aladdin* on his Nintendo.

So far, David had seen very few other people play the game. His older brother was a bit better at it than he was. I had caught the bug, and was about as good as the kids thanks to some late-night sessions after they had gone to bed. My wife steadfastly refused to play, on the reasonable grounds that it was a pointless waste of time.

But P, who had apparently never played a video game in her life, was a good sport and said she'd have a try. She started the first frame and immediately got killed. *Merde!* she said, and started again.

"You've got to jump like this," said David helpfully, trying to show her using body language. But his teaching method wasn't effective, and P kept on getting killed. *Merde! Merde! Merde!* she swore, as she failed to complete Level 1 for about the eighth time.

David looked at her, wondering what was going on, and suddenly the penny dropped. She wasn't pretending to make him feel good ... she actually couldn't do it!!! It was the first time he'd ever understood that he possessed a skill grown-ups lacked, and the realization was mind-blowing. He literally rolled around on the floor laughing for a couple of minutes. It's one of the few times I've seen this happen.

As Ewan McGregor says, we're not stupid you know.

Part II

Trash

Fear of Flying
Erica Jong

iw69: hello. i want you now

mannyrayner: do we know each other?

iw69: not at all, that's the point. i thought we could just have a completely no-strings-attached sexual encounter for its own sake and then say goodbye. wouldn't that be poetic and beautiful?

mannyrayner: um, well, maybe. i'm sorry, i guess i should just be doing this and not analyzing it. can i at least have a name or will that ruin everything?

iw69: i'm isadora

mannyrayner: that's a pretty name. pardon me for being so old-fashioned

iw69: it's ok. so now can we fuck?

mannyrayner: i'm not quite sure how that would work, but

iw69: i want you to put your hard cock in my cunt and make me come. i hope you aren't threatened by the way i frankly express my female desires or by my use of the word "cunt"?

mannyrayner: ah, no, not really, in fact i

iw69: it didn't used to be regarded as obscene. in the miller's tale, chaucer writes "pryvely he caught hir by the queynte." In 1380 "queynte" was pronounced "cunt"

mannyrayner: how interesting! i knew the line but wasn't aware of the pronunciation

iw69: and in swedish the root has mutated into the word "qvinna" which is the normal word for woman. so swedish women are all unashamedly cunts

mannyrayner: actually the word is normally spelled with a "k" in modern swedish, and the polite word for cunt is "sköte". you are not advised to use the vulgar "fitta"

iw69: you are remarkably knowledgeable. i already feel i understand you. you remind me of my first husband. i guess you're some kind of erratic genius type who's insecure about his sexuality and his ability to satisfy a woman, which is eventually going to destroy you?

mannyrayner: well, thanks for the first bit, but i hope you're not entirely

iw69: no wait, i think you're really more like my second husband. you're powerful and oversexed, but simultaneously cold and distant, so that while you satisfy my body you're unable to reach me emotionally?

mannyrayner: actually, i'm not sure i quite

iw69: you said "actually" again. you must be english, right? in fact, i see you're most like my lover adrian. you pretend to live in the moment, but all the time you have a plan you're hiding from me, which i'll be bitterly disappointed to discover in due course?

mannyrayner: i suppose i can't completely

iw69: hey, now i get it. you're like all of them at the same time. god you turn me on. i'm so wet from talking to you that i've had to change my panties twice already since the start of our conversation

mannyrayner: isadora, i admit i'm flattered, but

iw69: stay right where you are. i'll be with you faster than you would believe possible and then we're going to fuck like you've never fucked before in your whole life. you'll break my heart, but after i've dried my tears i'll put you and your cock in my next best-selling novel and you'll be immortal

mannyrayner: i guess i like some parts of the plan but we'll have to change a few details

iw69: why?

mannyrayner: to start with, i'm sitting in an airport lobby. i need to be at my gate within the next twenty minutes

mannyrayner: isadora?

mannyrayner: hello, are you still there?

mannyrayner: did i say something wrong?

mannyrayner: well, if it was zipless enough for you, then it was zipless enough for me

mannyrayner: bye!

Les liaisons dangereuses
Pierre Choderlos de Laclos

Letter 94. *Viscomte de Rayner to the Goodreads Community*

This morning, I thought of M. de Laclos's charming novel for the first time in years, when an interfering busybody saw fit to edit my Quiz question about it. I was forced to spend an hour checking the text, so that I could thoroughly refute her misconceptions about Cécile's role in the story, and I trust I shall hear no more from the vile creature. But, none the less, I am grateful to her, since she reminded me that I should read it in the original French. I fail to understand how I can have postponed this pleasant task so long.

Even in translation, *Les Liaisons Dangereuses* is marvellously entertaining, and not a little erotic. I well understand why that saucy minx Marie-Antoinette kept a copy by her bed! And it still speaks to all of us who enjoy meddling in the amorous affairs of others. I vividly recall watching Mr. Frears's fine moving picture version together with my friend, la Comtesse de B——. How we laughed, recalling our own machinations as we guided M. J—— through his fumbling relationship with Mlle. A——! Little did the two lovers know that their every tryst was promptly relayed, in written form, to an audience who, I believe, in some cases even were known to make wagers on the success or otherwise of M. J——'s strategems. A further piquancy was added by the fact that most of his ideas came directly from the Comtesse.

But I must not lose myself in past memories. It is already gone nine, and I have yet to write to my several mistresses, before I take my daily ride around the borders of my estate. I will need to advance my usual schedule a little, since I have a duel to fight in the early afternoon. Should I live (the contrary would be an unpleasant surprise; he is an abominably poor swordsman), I hope to continue this correspondence tomorrow.

Château de Cambridge
11 March, 20—

Megan's Mark
Lora Leigh

Every now and then, something happens to you that reaffirms your faith in the essential goodness of humanity. A few weeks ago, Choupette said she would like to get acquainted with the Brigade Mondaine series which I have been so diligently promoting in my reviews. I sent her a package of assorted Michel Brice. She asked if I wanted any contribution towards postage, but I told her that I believed that my karmic investment was clear, and I would surely get my reward in due course. I was just curious to know what form it would take.

And, less than two months later, I receive a package from Jordan containing this book and three similar ones! I remember telling her last year that *Twilight* was the only paranormal romance I'd ever read, and she had expressed concern. Now she's helped me fill this dreadful lacuna in my literary education ... I can't wait to start. Jordan, that was so nice of you. Call me a nut, call me a crazy dreamer, but I think that, if everyone in the world sent trashy erotic novels to their GoodReads friends in other countries, there would be no more war or poverty, and we could build a paradise in two generations. If you're one of the lucky people who has Barack Obama's new email address, you might want to pass that thought on to him.

The gap on my bookshelf left by my donation to Choupette was exactly the right size to hold Jordan's present. Truly, as it is written in the Good Book, cast thy Boris on the waters, and it shall return Lora Leigh.

I should say something about the book itself. It's billed as a steamy piece of women's erotica, and there's no doubt that it delivers. I had previously read almost no women's erotica at all (I'm sure there are people who are wondering how this is even possible), and on the whole I was pleasantly surprised. I thought it was more tasteful, more psychologically plausible, and more fun than its male counterpart.

It's notorious that women simply don't behave as they're supposed to do in male pornography; so, if you read it, you're creating a misleading image which can confuse you in all sorts of ways, some of them potentially very serious. Here, it didn't seem out of the question to believe that a woman could behave sexually the way Megan does. OK, she wants sex remarkably often, and it's amazing how much she enjoys it. Lucky Megan. But she's right at the start of a relationship with her super-hot dream guy, so yes, I thought this was possible. I found it harder to believe in Braden. He seemed a bit too much; too hot, too caring, too sensitive under that tough bad-boy exterior. So maybe *female* readers are getting themselves confused, and setting up false expectations that will disappoint *them* later. But hey, that's their problem. I'm just a male tourist, I don't live here.

The parts that weren't about sex didn't impress me too much. I thought Ms Leigh wasn't taking them very seriously, and they felt sloppily constructed. I can't resist mentioning a passage towards the end, which contains an extraordinary example of her flouting the Chekhov's Gun rule. Megan puts, not one, but TWO knives (sheathed) into her bra, before setting out on a hazardous expedition. I waited and waited. When would she use her pocket aces? Answer: NEVER! They didn't get used! The only point was to give the reader a cheap thrill when she put them in.

Since I have never worn a bra, much less put anything into it, I am the wrong person to comment, but I must say that it seemed like an extraordinarily uncomfortable fashion choice. I am prepared to be corrected on this.

Heretics of Dune
Frank Herbert

The guards ushered Frank into the office. As usual, the Reverend Publisher was seated at her desk, writing.

So many lives touched by her decisions, he thought.

"Well?"

She looked up. He had promised himself that he would not flinch before the fire of her gaze, and once more he broke his promise.

"It is ... almost finished."

"Almost." Her irony was palpable, a force. "Almost is not enough. You know that, Frank. When will it be done?"

"I think ... a month. At most two. I am working as hard as I can, Reverend Publisher. I am ... not well."

He hated himself for his servility.

"So, why then did you found a dynasty? Your son can assist you. He will continue when you are gone. There are many books left to write."

His throat was suddenly dry. But of course there was no pitcher of water. It would have been unthinkable.

"I am ... preparing him. He will be ready in time."

She glanced at him again, and again he flinched.

"There is a transcriber on that desk. Write a page now. I want to see how you work."

He sat down, and fed a sheet of paper into the machine. His lips moved soundlessly. She knew what he was saying. By now, the Litany was stamped deep into his psyche, impossible to eradicate. She smiled secretly to herself. The training was brutal, but it was effective. She watched his mouth, as it formed the words it had spoken so many times before:

> *I have no taste.*
> *Taste is the sales-killer, the hesitation that brings total profit meltdown.*
> *I will conquer my taste.*
> *When I have stamped it out, I will look at what I have written.*
> *I will read through it from start to finish.*
> *There will be nothing left of a great series.*
> *Only crap will remain.*

Hoki: A Manny Rayner novel based on Shibumi
Trevanian

The bell rang three times, two short and one long. It was the signal they'd agreed on.

"*Entrez!*" said Rayner. "*La porte est ouverte.*"

The man entered hesitantly, looking around with evident curiosity at the apartment's simple but costly furnishings. An elderly Chinese servant glided up to him, discreetly took his heavy winter coat, and left again without uttering a word. The man cleared his throat.

"*Ah ... vous êtes ...*"

His accent was as atrociously American as the rest of him. Rayner permitted himself an inward smile.

"We can talk English if you prefer."

"Gee ... that might be easier. My French isn't too hot. Lucky Geneva is so international."

Rayner said nothing. The man would soon come out with his crass, commercial proposition. These people were all the same.

"Well ... guess time is money and all that, so why don't I cut to the chase. We might have a job for you."

Rayner breathed out slowly, already planning his next moves. The dialogue was as easy to predict as the main line of the *tsuke-nobi joseki*.

"I might be interested. It would depend on what it was."

"I represent a ... powerful organization. There's a ... book we need reviewed. We're willing to pay."

"You're from Goodreads, and you want me to review *Shibumi*," said Rayner. It was not a question.

The American blinked, unable to hide his surprise.

"You're well informed. That's right."

"Please tell me more."

"Okay, it's like this..." began the American, and then stopped abruptly as a sublimely beautiful woman entered the room. She was carrying a silver tray with a teapot and three Sèvres cups, which she gracefully set down on the low table between the two men.

"You may continue," said Rayner, as his guest paused, uncertain what to do. "Mademoiselle Not enjoys my full confidence."

"Right," said the American, unable to take his eyes off the woman. "Like I said, we need a review. We can offer you fifty thousand dollars for a quick turnaround."

"Two hundred," said Rayner. "And Swiss Francs."

A flash of anger crossed the American's face. "That's a lot. We have other people who could do this..."

"I'm sure you do," said Rayner gravely. "I hear Brisette, for example, is a Go player with strong linguistic skills. Why not give it to her?"

The American banged his fist on the table. "Look," he began, but Rayner was no longer listening. Something was wrong. Suddenly, he leapt to his feet and launched himself at his guest, sending him crashing to the floor. An instant later, the *shuriken* whistled through the space the American's head had just occupied and embedded itself in the wall. Rayner continued his dive, rolling smoothly as he simultaneously snatched one of the cups. Then, in a blur of speed, he projected it towards the open window.

A black-clad figure tumbled into the room, the tea-cup handle cleanly transfixing his neck. The American stared, hardly able to believe what had happened.

"So that was ..."

"*Hoda korosu*," said Rayner. "Naked kill. And, unless I am much mistaken, Amazon are also interested in this project."
(Continued for another 499 pages)

Sarah

Marek Halter

The Book of Marek

1. Now in those days there dwelled in the land of the France'ites a man named Ma'rek, who was a prophet of the Lord.

2. And Ma'rek had suffered much for his faith and undergone many trials. And he had seen how strange are the Lord's ways.

3. Now Ma'rek had need of gold. And he prayed to the Lord, saying, show me how I might get me riches, that I may further exalt Thy name.

4. Then that night an angel came to Ma'rek in a dream. And the angel said, write thou a history of Abraham's wife, that is called Sarah, and tell Abraham's story as she did see it; this is the Lord's command.

5. And Ma'rek was afeared, and he said, I am a man; how may I write as a woman? For I know nothing of periods, or pregnancies or other lady business. And moreover, there is little in the Lord's book touching his daughter Sarah, and how may I speak of things I know not? For surely that would anger the Lord.

6. But the angel said, still thy fear; I will instruct thee in all these matters, and tell unto thee Sarah's secret story, that has been lost for many years. Write thou as I speak, and all will be well.

7. And the angel said, thou knowest already that Sarah was the fairest of women. Write first how she was formed: that she had long curvy eyelashes, and fabulous tits, and a deliciously flat stomach, and a hot, tight little ... well, thou gettest the picture.

8. Alleluia.

9. And then shalt thou write of Sarah's early years, before

she did join her busband in holy matrimony; how she was the Chosen of the Goddess Ishtar, and did sexy topless dances where she sacrificed bulls in Ishtar's temple. For strange are the ways of the Lord, as already noted.

10. And when Sarah did meet Hagar, the daughter of Pharaoh, write thou of how Hagar did strip Sarah naked, and herself also, and did give her hot girl-on-girl massage in a bath of asses' milk. For thus was it, though none did know until this day.

11. And many more naughty details shall I vouchsafe thee, that thy book be a page-turner which all men do read.

12. And Ma'rek was amazed, but he did write as the angel told him. And he did go to the publisher. And the publisher spake, saying, dude, I love it. We got ourselves a winner.

13. And Ma'rek's book was published, and did sell many myriads of copies; even in airport bookstalls was it sold. And across the land of the France'ites was there wailing and gnashing of teeth when the wise men of that land did read it.

14. But Ma'rek cared not what the wise men said, for he knew he did the Lord's work. And verily did he receive much gold, yea, he did laugh all the way to the bank.

15. Here endeth the book of Ma'rek.

Skye O'Malley
Bertrice Small

Bad Book Is Bad, Scientists Say

A team of top researchers from the prestigious Goodreads Institute of Bodice-Ripping Studies have recently published a report concluding that a bad book is bad.

"We were very surprised when we analysed the data," said the Institute's charismatic director at yesterday's press conference. "We had expected this bad book to be, you know, good in places, or perhaps a bit amusing. Instead, it contains bad writing, bad character development, bad sex and a bad plot. In a word, it's bad. But that won't stop us reading another 214 bad books, or as many as it takes to establish, to a high level of statistical significance, our controversial thesis that bad books are often bad."

A specially trained psychic tried to contact the late Dr. B. Fish for comments, but at press time was still unable to reach him due to technical problems involving a massive black hole.

Devil of the Highlands
Lynsay Sands

Freak Talent Baffles Researchers

Scientists at the world-famous Goodreads Institute of Bodice-Ripping Studies say they are "baffled" by a man who is able to evaluate a book simply by picking it up and riffling through it for five seconds.

"It's uncanny," said a senior researcher, speaking under condition of anonymity, "and we still don't know how he does it. Take this one, for example. As everyone knows, you can't judge a book by its cover. I look at it, and all I see is a paperback with a picture of an attractive, half-naked man on the front. I open it at random and look at the first word that catches my eye, which happens to be 'nipple'. What conclusions can I draw from that? Nothing. I'd have to read the book from cover to cover, working hard to build up a complex picture of plot, style, thematic elements and literary influences. Somehow, he just immediately knows it's a trashy romance. He's some kind of *idiot savant*, but we wish we could say more than that."

Jemima Puddleduck meets a French trash novel

Beatrix Potter and Michel Brice

Naked, Jémima swam to the bank and, in one sinuous motion, emerged from the water. She stood for a moment and gazed at the reflection mirrored in the pond's smooth surface.

Pas mal, she thought, *pas mal du tout!* An elegant, sensuous bill, slick white feathers over a delicately rounded breast, deliciously stubby little legs. Without thinking, she brushed one wing down the length of her body, stopping only when it reached the insistently upturned tail ...

And then she saw her clothes, lying among the reeds where she had carelessly flung them half an hour earlier, and her heart filled with rage. A decrepit, worn-out old shawl and a bonnet that might perhaps have been fashionable when her mother was a young duckling. Who would ever want her, when every stitch she wore screamed that she was a poor, worthless bird, fit only for laying eggs and an occasional brief swim on her morning off?

Le fric, she said bitterly to herself. *Toujours le fric.* If only she could make some money, get herself a better wardrobe, move to a decent nest. But no, to make money you need to have money. She was 19 years old, and already she felt trapped.

"Ahem ... "

Jémima suddenly became aware that she was not alone. A handsome gentleman with a foxy air and red whiskers was standing close to her, unashamedly looking her up and down. She blushed, instinctively pulling her shawl closer around her.

"I am sorry — I did not mean to startle Mademoiselle. I cannot help feeling that she would be perfect in my new TV show. But, no doubt her parents would not permit it ... "

His voice was thrillingly low, and sent a frisson of excitement coursing through Jémima's blood. Could this be it? The chance she'd been waiting for so long? She did her best to return the gentleman's frank look.

"They won't mind. They — they respect my freedom."

She stumbled over the words, almost quacking in her eagerness to appear as suave and sophisticated as her new acquaintance. But he did not seem to notice.

"In that case, may I be so bold as to invite Mademoiselle to lunch at my apartment? So that we can discuss the proposition at our leisure?"

He smiled at her, exposing long white teeth.

"*Avec — avec plaisir,*" stammered Jémima. Wasn't that what one said?

The gentleman smiled again. "If Mademoiselle does not mind, we will just make a short stop at the grocery store first," he said. "I need to buy a few things ... some pancakes, and perhaps a little plum sauce ..."

Jémima followed him docilely to his car. She could still hardly believe this was happening to her.

Breaking Dawn
Stephenie Meyer

I am shocked, dismayed, not surprised at all to discover from Usually Reliable Sources that the series has a happy ending. Let's recap. The story so far: Bella, a shy, bookish, unimaginative 17 year old girl who's never been kissed, falls in love with Edward, who once was human but has now been transformed, by means not fully explained in the books, into a robot-like being with an insatiable craving for blood. Edward tries to control every aspect of Bella's life, including stealing into her bedroom at night and watching over her while she sleeps. At one point, Edward leaves Bella abruptly, pushing her into a state of suicidal despair. He in fact believes, on rather slender evidence, that she has killed herself, and, rather than trying to find out whether she really is dead, decides to kill himself too. Bella, who has not died, is forced to risk her life a second time to save his.

While Edward was out of the picture, Bella has fallen in love with Jacob, who reciprocates her feelings. After she gets back together with Edward, she callously abandons Jacob, mirroring Edward's behavior towards her. Edward then cleverly manipulates both Bella and Jacob to destroy her relationship with the one person who truly loves and cares for her. He also uses Bella's feelings of sexual attraction towards him to trick her into marrying him, something Bella has made quite clear that she does not want to do. At the end of Book 3, Bella is being coerced into a wedding she hates the very idea of. Once they are married, Edward is going to turn her into a creature similar to himself. This means that she will also be a blood-craving robot, and will never be able to have children. It is also likely that their union will trigger a major war between Edward's and Jacob's families.

We are clearly being set up for a geek *[Surely "Greek"? Ed.]*

tragedy, and a logical ending might have been something like the following. Bella's and Edward's wedding proceeds as planned under Alice's manic supervision. On their wedding night, Edward makes a last-ditch attempt to persuade Bella not to have sex with him while still human. She refuses, and holds him to his promise. The sex is excruciatingly painful and nearly fatal; in order to save her life, Edward is forced to turn Bella into a vampire there and then. As a new-born, Bella lacks all self-control. During the early hours of the morning, she sneaks out of the bridal suite, lured by an overwhelmingly enticing smell. The trail leads to her mother's room; evidently, Bella's delicious scent has been genetically inherited. She breaks down the door, and kills and eats Renee. Then, overcome by remorse, she flees alone into the wilderness.

Jacob hears about the ghastly events, and deduces what has happened. Edward has violated the terms of the werewolf/vampire treaty, and Jacob is also consumed by rage and jealousy. He summons the werewolf pack, and they attack the Cullen residence in force. Bella has realised, too late, that he will do this. She hastens to Forks, but arrives when the battle is already in full swing. Sam kills Carlisle and Esme, before himself being killed by Jasper. Edward and Jacob kill each other in single combat. Bella looks on, horrified and grief-stricken, but is powerless to intervene.

At this point, the Volturi arrive. It turns out that Bella, in her new vampire form, is no longer immune to the demonic Jane. Jane paralyzes her, and forces her to watch as the Volturi kill the remaining Cullens and werewolves. Finally, when everyone else lies dead and dismembered on the ground, Jane is kind enough to kill her too.

But, instead ... no, I can't continue. What the hell, Stephenie Meyer is right! To show how whole-heartedly I embrace her solution, here's my improved ending to *Hamlet*. We join the action in the middle of the fencing match between Hamlet and

Laertes from Act V, Scene 2.

HAMLET: I'll play this bout first; set it by awhile. Come.

They play

Another hit; what say you?

LAERTES: A touch, a touch, I do confess.

KING CLAUDIUS: Our son shall win.

A pause. Then:

LAERTES: I can't do it. It's wrong. I'm sorry, man.

He throws down the foil

LAERTES: Hamlet, you may be a vampire, but you're my friend.

HAMLET: You may be a werewolf, but I love you.

LAERTES and HAMLET embrace

GERTRUDE: I'll drink to that.

CLAUDIUS: Don't ... ah, shit, too late.

Enter POLONIUS

POLONIUS: Fear not, I switched the cups.

HAMLET: Huh? But ... you're dead. I killed you.

POLONIUS: Just a flesh wound. I thought it would be safer to be out of the picture for a while.

HAMLET: Gee, you're smarter than I thought. You'd have made a great father-in-law, if only ...

Enter OPHELIA, carrying a MUTANT VAMPIRE BABY

OPHELIA: Hi honey! This is Renesmee. But I call her Nessie. You're her father.

HAMLET: Oh, uh ... good. If only my own father were still ...

CLAUDIUS wipes the makeup from his face, and we see he is

really HAMLET'S FATHER in disguise
HAMLET: ... Dad?
HAMLET'S FATHER: Son!
They embrace
HAMLET: But ...
HAMLET'S FATHER: I wanted to see if you really cared about me.
HAMLET: Um ... I nearly stabbed you once when you were praying, you know.
HAMLET'S FATHER: I don't think that would have worked.
He opens his robes to reveal a Kevlar vest
HAMLET: Oh, wow, this is like ... incredible. Group hug!
HAMLET, HAMLET'S FATHER, GERTRUDE, LAERTES, POLONIUS, OPHELIA and OPHELIA'S MUTANT VAMPIRE BABY all embrace
HORATIO: *[who has somehow been left out]* Why does the drum come hither?
March within. Enter FORTINBRAS, the English Ambassadors, and others.
FORTINBRAS: What is this sight?
HORATIO: Well may you ask. It's a long story.
He starts whispering in FORTINBRAS's ear. FORTINBRAS mimes astonishment, disbelief, outrage etc as the curtain falls.
FINIS

I suppose I'll still have to read it. But under protest, as one might say.

OK, I've read it, so now I'm speaking from a position of both knowledge and prejudice, rather than just prejudice. I hope everyone grasps the subtle distinction.

Well ... the first two thirds aren't bad. Her technical writing skills have improved since *Twilight*, and the atmosphere was suitably menacing and creepy. She did a good job of maintaining the ambiguity, so that we weren't sure about how reliable Bella was as a narrator. I approved of the way she treated the sex during their honeymoon. Bella, who's usually so appallingly, prosaically circumstantial about the smallest details, suddenly can't remember a thing about it, although there are bruises all over her body and Edward is in shock about what he's done to her. You do wonder what's going on. Try as I will, I find it difficult to imagine how a human woman could ever enjoy sex with a cold, robot-like vampire. But they have mind-control powers, some of which (Jasper's, for example) work on Bella, so it's entirely possible that she's somehow being manipulated. And the following part, where the mutant child starts growing and sucking the life from her body, is effective too. Bella's utter irrationality is scary, as is the Alien-like thing inside her. The horrifying birth scene is one of Meyer's best passages.

But then ... oh dear. If anything, my *Hamlet* parody understated the extent of the difficulties she runs into. I have nothing against the *deus ex machina* as a plot device. Heck, if it's good enough for Shakespeare and Molière, it's good enough for Stephenie Meyer. The problem here is that she's ignoring all the basic rules. To start off with, she doesn't just have one *deus ex machina*; she has at least two big ones (Jacob imprinting on Renesmee, and the sudden production of the other half-immortal), plus some smaller ones (Bella's new abilities as a shield, and the switch of position regarding werewolves).

Also, the *deus ex machina* is normally used at the end, not in the middle, and it works best in the context of a comedy. Think of Frank Oz's version of *Little Shop of Horrors*, one of my favorite black comedies. Having Seymour electrocute the Plant and live happily ever after with Audrey works fine. You know perfectly well that he's really been eaten, just as you know perfectly well that *Tartuffe* really ends with poor Orgon being turned out of his own home. Here, though, with the *dei ex machina* coming down like hail all through Part 3, you don't know what to think. She actually seems to believe in her illogical happy ending rather than just intending it ironically. All the dramatic tension disappears. It's such a waste of a great build-up.

And, before I go back to reading the conclusion of *Mysterier*, a final thought about the absurd vampire science. If I understand correctly, the hocus-pocus with the numbers of chromosomes in the different species is there to establish the validity of the key equation

$$\text{Werewolf} = \frac{1}{2}(\text{Human} + \text{Vampire})$$

If Renesmee weren't a kind of werewolf, Jacob wouldn't have been able to imprint on her. But did anyone stop to consider that you can rearrange the terms to get the following form?

$$\text{Human} = 2 \times \text{Werewolf} - \text{Vampire}$$

I'll leave you to ponder the significance of that.

Part III

Literachuh

En attendant Godot
Samuel Beckett

ACT III

VLADIMIR: They've called us back.
ESTRAGON: For an encore?
VLADIMIR: No, we're supposed to say what it means.
[A pause]
ESTRAGON: What what means?
VLADIMIR: This play! We have to explain it.
ESTRAGON: And then?
VLADIMIR: *[discouraged]* I don't know. Maybe Godot will arrive. But again, maybe he won't. He's not very reliable. *[Another pause]* Still, we can try.
[They both think deeply]
VLADIMIR: Any ideas yet?
ESTRAGON: My boots don't fit. My feet hurt.
VLADIMIR: *[furious]* Idiot! This isn't about your boots. We're talking meaning here! Philosophy!
ESTRAGON: Sorry.
[They continue to think. Enter POZZO and LUCKY]
VLADIMIR: Ah! How fortunate. Maybe you can explain the meaning of this play?
POZZO: My sight has been miraculously restored.
VLADIMIR: Oh! Good. But ...
POZZO: Lucky!
[LUCKY moves center stage, and begins mumbling in a flat monotone voice]

LUCKY: Man's search for himself in an inhospitable cosmos ... absurdity of all human action ... black humour ... marked by his wartime experiences ...

[POZZO punches him, knocking LUCKY down]

LUCKY: *[writhing on the ground]* ... shifting relationship between the signifier and the signified ...

[POZZO continues to kick him savagely]

LUCKY: *[gasping]* ... différance ... impossibility of interpretation ... semiotics ... encoding ... oh fuck! ... fuck! ... please stop kicking me! I don't know! I don't know!

POZZO: *[finally smiling]* That's better.

1984 meets Lolita
George Orwell and Vladimir Nabokov

— You sent for me, sir?

— Yes. Smith, Winston?

— That's right sir.

— Alright, Smith, sit down. I have an assignment for you. It's a little unusual.

— Yes sir.

— How do you feel about pedophiles, Smith?

— Well sir ...

— You hate them, right?

— Yes sir. If that's what the Party wants me to do.

— Well it does. Make no mistake about that. We have too many pedophiles running around, and we want less of them.

— Yes sir. I feel the same way sir.

— So we want you to be heading up our new anti-pedophile campaign.

— Thank you sir. It's an honor. I'm thinking, a few public executions, a ...

— No, Smith. That's not what we want. Please remind me of our basic principles here.

— Well sir, love is hate, truth is lies, war ...

— Exactly, Smith. We don't want public executions. We want a novel that presents pedophilia in a positive light.

— I'm sorry sir?

— We want the narrator to be a charming, witty pedophile, who'll seduce his readers into thinking that pedophilia actually isn't that bad.

— Ah, yes sir. I'm not quite sure where this is going yet ...

— Smith, your immediate superior told me you were quick on the uptake. Please don't make me discipline him.

— Well sir, ah, perhaps it would become apparent later in the novel that the narrator wasn't such an, ah, admirable person after all?

— Good. Please go on.

— And that pedophilia was actually a reprehensible activity?

— Indeed.

— And the reader's revulsion would be all the greater because they had earlier sympathized with the narrator?

— Not too bad, Smith, though you could definitely be quicker. Do you have anyone in your section who could write this?

— Sir, I think Nabokov could do it. He writes quite well. I think he's underutilized on war propaganda.

— Have him start tomorrow. Tell him it's urgent.

— Yes sir.

— What should we do with him when he's finished?

— Ah, well sir, I'm not sure ...

— Is he a Party member?

— No sir.

— Does he generally follow the Party line politically?

— I'm not really certain of that sir.

— Well, I think the usual solution then.

— I'm sorry sir?

— Unpersoned, doubleplusquickwise. I'm disappointed in you, Smith. I shouldn't need to spell this out.

— I'm sorry sir. Sir, are you sure we couldn't just send him to Switzerland? In practice, it's almost the same as unpersoning.

— Are you trying to be amusing, Smith?

— No sir.

— Maybe it's worth consideration. It could be cheaper.

— Yes sir.

— Very well, I expect his novel on my desk by the first of next month.

— It will be, sir.

— Make sure it is. Dismissed.

À la recherche du temps perdu
Marcel Proust

When you read Proust, and learn to appreciate his extraordinary, dreamy, hypnotic, truly inimitable style (this review is a mere shadow on the wall of a Platonic cave), which succeeds in making the syntax of language, usually as invisible as air, into a tangible element, so that, like literary yogis, we may feel, for the first time, how enjoyable the simple activity of reading, like breathing, can be; and discover the delights of sentences which took the author days to construct and us an hour to read, unpacking layers of subordinate clauses to discover, nestling inside their crisp folds, a simile as unexpected and delicious as a Swiss chocolate rabbit, wearing a yellow marzipan waistcoat and carrying an edible rake, found in its cocoon of tissue paper under a lilac bush during a childhood Easter egg hunt; or, steaming across the calm waters of a limpid grammatical lake in the capable hands of Captain Marcel and his crew, confident that they know the route from generations of experience, and will in due time, exactly on schedule, arrive at the main verb, pointing us tourists to it with justifiable, understated pride; then you will gradually come to identify with the alchemical author, spending twenty years sitting, propped up by pillows, in his velvet dressing-gown, transmuting the lead of his accumulated experience into gold, surrounded by galley proofs which he constantly rereads and revises, pasting in a parenthesis in the middle of this sentence, an apposition in that, so that the papers are gradually festooned, like bizarre Christmas decorations, with loops and curlicues of afterthoughts; and waiting for life, his unfaithful mistress, to leave him, simultaneously knowing that it is inevitable, and also that she will never do so, at least as long as this, the greatest and strangest of all novels, is still not quite finished ...

Paradise Lost
John Milton

— George?

— Mm?

— I had such a strange dream.

— Was it scary? You were talking in your sleep.

— Michael Bay and Jerry Bruckheimer were making a movie of *Paradise Lost*.

— OK, that's scary.

— Bay was showing the rushes to Bruckheimer.

— Mm-hm.

— So first he was teasing him and pretending it was some kind of arthouse movie. He was showing the beginning where you just could see the Garden of Eden and nothing was happening and Anthony Hopkins was reading aloud from Milton.

— Did Bruckheimer think that was funny?

— No, no, not at all! He looked like he was almost in pain and kept moaning "Mike, how could you do this to me?"

— Ah. I was wondering who Mike was.

— I was saying that in my sleep?

— I'm afraid you were.

— How embarrassing! Anyway, then the camera panned round and we could see he'd cast Megan Fox as Eve. She was running in slo-mo like she does in that bit from *Transformers 2*, except that she wasn't wearing anything.

— How come *I* never see Megan Fox nude in my dreams? But I guess that cheered Bruckheimer up a bit?

— Well, he still looked grumpy. He muttered something about didn't she say Bay was like Hitler. You remember, that interview she did?

— And what did Bay say?

— He gave Bruckheimer this soulful look and said "Megan and I understand each other."

— Ha! So if Megan is Eve, who's Adam?

— Bay has cast Robert Pattinson. You know, Edward from *Twilight*, and he's also running along wearing nothing at all.

— So now Bruckheimer must be pleased?

— Oh yes, but he's worried about the nudity, he thinks it's too much. So Bay shows him this other take where you can't see anything, like in *Austin Powers*. Bruckheimer says that's better.

— Your dreams are always so amazingly circumstantial!

— Well I'm a very circumstantial kind of person.

— You are. It's one of your best features. So then what happened?

— Um, they were looking at some other scenes, and Bruckheimer kept complaining that there was too much poetry and no one would understand the language.

— He might have a point there.

— Oh, I don't think it's that difficult. And Bay was saying come on Jerry, think Passion of the Christ, think Apocalypto, think Inglourious Basterds ...

— I suppose you could use subtitles.

— Yes, that's just what Bruckheimer suggested too. And they were cutting out all my favorite scenes and saying no, it's too talky, they won't like this.

— So what do they have left?

— Well there is a lot of sex and violence you know. Bay was showing Bruckheimer the battle sequence where Messiah is routing the forces of evil ...

— Who had he cast as Messiah?

— Arnold Schwarzenegger. He had this big laser gun or something, and he was blasting away at the fallen angels, except they looked like Decepticons ...

— I guess a Decepticon is a kind of fallen angel when you think about it? And Optimus Prime is a Christ figure, isn't he? I'm sure I read that somewhere ...

— I suppose he is. Anyway, Arnie's blatting the Decepticons to hell ...

— Literally.

— Oh, quite literally. And he's shouting "Eat wrath-of-God, muthafuckas!"

— I take it that was an ad lib? It doesn't really sound like Milton.

— Yes, Bay and Bruckheimer were arguing about whether to keep it or not. And if they should give Arnie a halo. Bruckheimer said the religious right would like that.

— Um, they might. But they might think it was blasphemous too. So wait, we have Megan Fox as Eve, Robert Pattinson as Adam and Arnie as Christ, but who's playing Satan?

— Ah, well first I think it was Daniel Craig ...

— As in *The Golden Compass*? Lord Azreal is clearly Satan, right?

— Yes, exactly, but then somehow he turned into Michael Douglas. So, damn, I'm already starting to forget what happened, but there was this scene from Book 2 where he meets Sin ...

— Who's she?

— Glenn Close, who else? She looked like Cruella de Vil from *101 Dalmations*. He doesn't recognize her, but she reminds him that they used to be a hot item, and then there was this flashback to them having sex over the sink, as in *Fatal Attraction* ...

— I don't think that's in Milton either?

— Well, not the sink. Anyway, Bay and Bruckheimer are arguing about will the 16-24 demographic get it and should Glenn Close boil Megan Fox's bunny ...

— I think she should.

— Yes, I thought so too. And then there's this commotion outside, and the door flies open, and in comes Tilda Swinton dressed as the White Witch.

— Lilith? That's kind of thematic, in fact. So what did she do?

— She took out her wand, and shouted "Eve was framed!" and zapped Bay and Bruckheimer into snakes. They were slithering around on the floor hissing, it was quite horrible. And then I woke up.

— Wow. You should write this down before you forget it. Like Coleridge.

— I might. But first I think we should snuggle a bit more. So I forget about those snakes at least. And George?

— Mm?

— You're much nicer than the Person from Porlock.

The Crying of Lot 49
Thomas Pynchon

"So, what do you think it's about?" she asked, as she took a preliminary sip from her cocktail. "Entropy, to start with," he replied. "If only he'd known the Holographic Principle. It follows from thermodynamic calculations that the information content of a black hole is proportional to the square of its radius, not the cube, and the Universe can reasonably be thought of as a black hole. Hence all its information is really on its surface, and the interior is a low-energy illusion. Wouldn't you say that the book is rather like that too?"

"Mm-hm," she said, wondering if she should make a pun about quantum gravity and rainbows, but thinking better of it. "And then the deficiencies of the Container Metaphor of Communication," he continued. "On the naïve view, information is put into a container, namely the words, delivered to the addressee by the US mailman, and opened to obtain the meaning. But real communication is more informal. It's pieces of courier post from an unknown sender that arrive in turn, in taxis."

"Thurn and Taxis?" she interrupted. He looked at her for a moment.

"We could have sex," he added, in a tone midway between an afterthought, a question and a declaration of religious belief. She sighed, and undid the top two buttons of her blouse; he noticed they had a hard-edged quality different from the lower ones. A gold pendant, surprised by the sudden daylight and unsuccessfully attempting to hide between her breasts, spelled out the W.A.S.T.E. symbol. He examined it carefully, then hoisted the focus of his attention back towards her face. She made a complicated gesture, simultaneously expressing her agreement with the essential reasonableness of his request and the impossibility of acquiescing, then did up her blouse again.

"I think another martini would be useful," she said. "But this time, I want to see how you pit the olives. How you extract the kernel, as it were." She followed his hands as they cooperated in this task, which she had always felt beyond her. The left hand steadied the olive between thumb and forefinger, while the right one held the knife, exerting a steady downward pressure. The agate-coloured flesh split neatly apart, revealing the unwanted stone, which the right hand then discarded.

"Now let me try," she said, but she knew that, as usual, it would not work. Somehow, she was holding it in the wrong way; she only managed to inflict a flesh wound, rather than his clean kill. She relinquished the knife, and allowed him to do the remaining olives.

At least she had her martini, even if its secret still eluded her.

Good Omens meets Madame Bovary
Terry Pratchett, Neil Gaiman and Gustave Flaubert

I somehow ended up reading them both simultaneously. So I couldn't help wondering

What Madam Bovary Might Have Thought Of Good Omens

Three days later, a package arrived; there was no return address, but she immediately recognised Rodolphe's hand. It contained a paperback novel, whose title was *Good Omens*. Feverishly, she cast herself over it. Her English was poor, but, with the aid of a dictionary, she persevered and soon made great progress.

The more she read, the greater her bewilderment became. The book at first reminded her of *Candide*, which she had surreptitiously read at the convent, but M. Voltaire's *ésprit* had been replaced by another ingredient she was unable to name; she suspected that it must be the strange English invention they called *humour*. All the personages were well-meaning and agreeable; the witches, the torturers of witches, the prostitutes, even the Demons of Hell; they were filled with kindness and compassion, and their worst faults amounted to an occasional mild irritability. Where were the indifference and thoughtless cruelty that surrounded her, and which had now become the very air she breathed?

She did not know whether Rodolphe had sent her the book to comfort her or to mock her in her despair, and her futile attempts to resolve this question gradually resulted in an agonising headache. Her husband prescribed an infusion of valerian, and persuaded her to retire for the night; she lay sleepless in her bed a long time, until the drug finally took effect just as the sky was beginning to lighten. She dreamed of apocalyptic prophecies, red-headed women wielding swords, endless circles of horseless carriages, young boys with dogs.

In the morning, she remembered that she should purchase some arsenic.

It seemed unfair for this to be one-way. So, in the spirit of granting a right of reply, here's

What Good Omens Might Have Thought Of Madam Bovary

"I saw this smashin' film yesterday on TV," said Adam, as the Them listened attentively. "It was called Madam Bovver-Boy —"

"She was a lady skinhead?" interrupted Brian.

"No, stupid," said Adam. "It's a French name. *Bovver-Boy. By Flow-Bear.*"

"You mean Madame Bovary, by Flaubert," said Wensleydale. "I read about it in The Encyclopaedia of World Literature."

Adam gave him a withering glance. "That's what I said," he continued. "Madam Bovver-Boy, by Flow-Bear. She's married to this doctor, and he's dead borin', so she starts hangin' around with these two lovers, and then she maxes out her credit card, so she eats arsernick and poisons herself. The bit where she's dyin' of the arsernick is dead good. Her tongue's hanging out and she's screamin' —"

"Why did she max out her credit card?" asked Pepper.

"She was buying presents for her lovers," said Adam. "Roses an' boxes of chocolates an' stuff like that —"

"I thought the lovers were supposed to give her presents?" said Brian dubiously. "My sister's boyfriend gave her this huge bunch of roses on Valentine's Day, and a box of Quality Street, and a balloon with —"

"She gave them presents instead because it was a proto-feminist novel," explained Wensleydale authoritatively. "That's what The Encyclopaedia of World Literature says."

Adam felt that his control of the situation was slipping, and decided to up the stakes. "It's all true," he said, in an exegetical move that would have had Flaubert scholars around the world clutching their foreheads. "*Based* on a true story," he added prudently, in case the The Encyclopaedia of World Literature happened to have opinions on the subject.

Behind the bushes, Aziraphale raised an eyebrow. Crowley looked defensive. "Very loosely based," he whispered hastily. "I mean, I tempted her, it's my job you know, but Gustave changed the ending for dramatic purposes. Said it didn't work to have Rodolphe sort out her debts and then settle down in a cozy *ménage à quatre* with her, Léon and her husband. I told him that's what actually happened, but he insisted the arsenic worked better ..."

The Picture of Dorian Gray
Oscar Wilde

"My dear Jordan!" said Lord Rayner expansively, as the butler discreetly closed the door behind his young visitor. "Really, it is too good to see you again! And what brings you to Cambridge?"

"Oh, this and that," said the lad, flinging himself casually onto a priceless Ikea divan. "By the way, has there been some mistake in the casting? I thought I was female?"

"Well, since we're doing *Dorian Gray*, I hoped you would have no objection to reversing your gender," said his host. "And besides, is there anything quite as female as an attractive young man?"

"How could one disagree?" murmured the lad, as a becoming blush suffused his ivory cheek. "So, aren't you glad I persuaded you to read it?"

"In fact," said Lord Rayner, "I realised after a few pages that I already had read it, just not in one piece. It is almost too quotable. But I found it interesting to discover in which order the lines were meant to occur. Anyway, why don't we start writing our review?"

He opened the filigree-encrusted laptop, and, with his long, pianist's fingers, grasped the Louis-Quinze mouse, causing the bejewelled cursor to dance around the crystalline screen. "Now, where shall we begin?"

"I was wondering if you'd find it too gay?" hazarded the lad.

"Fortunately," said his Lordship, as he typed into the review box on the exquisitely crafted website, "I am quite straight. Had I been the slightest bit gay, I would not have been able to get the distance required to appreciate this unquestioned masterpiece of homoerotic art. But I am forgetting my manners.

Could I offer you some refreshment? I happen to have a case of 1997 Pepsi, which I had been saving for a special occasion."

"By all means," said the lad, as he idly revised a few words in Lord Rayner's text.

"Pepsi!" sighed the lord, as he poured the murky beverage into two delicate, long-stemmed glasses. "Its charm resides, does it not, in its wonderful uniformity? Every Pepsi is exactly the same as every other. I wager that you cannot perceive the slightest difference between this and the 2004 we enjoyed last month, and yet we both have the delightful thrill of knowing that they are distinct. It is a less intense form of the pleasure I experience when I betray my mistress with her twin sister."

"You always pretend to be so very bad!" laughed the youth. "Yet I am sure that you are really much better than that."

"On the contrary," said Lord Rayner gravely, "I am much worse. And was that not actually Basil's line?"

"I am afraid," said the youth, "that Basil is unable to join us this evening."

There was a moment of silence.

"So," continued the lad, "let us return to the review. Should we say something more about the construction? For example, did you not sometimes feel that it was rather trivial to reduce the deep questions of life to a series of throwaway epigrams?"

"My dear Jordan," said Lord Rayner, "The epigrams are the only serious part of the book. The rest is at best melodramatic nonsense. But I agree, you do have a point. His paradoxes are too logical, too systematic ... in a word, too French. What the book needs is a little English irrationality every now and then."

"But," pursued his young friend, "even though the author explicitly refused to allow the possibility that his art could be naturalistic, I did find it difficult to suspend disbelief at times.

Can one really pretend that people talk like this?"

"Alas," said the lord, "it is exactly there that the author has failed. Ever since Wilde, the British educated classes find it impossible to talk in any other way."

A melodious phrase interrupted him. Jordan started, then pulled out his quattrocento iPhone, which was insistently playing the opening bars of Mozart's concerto for piano and violin. He glanced at it, and rose apologetically.

"I'm terribly sorry, but I must go," he stammered. "Only, before I do, I have ... a question. Your avatar ... I know for a fact that you are 51, and yet your picture still shows you, unchanged, exactly as you were when you were 45. How is this possible?"

A strange look came over Lord Rayner's face. "Ah," he said, "it is a long story ... "

The Trial
Franz Kafka

The tortured bureaucratic world described in *The Trial* always strikes me as startlingly modern. I wondered

How *The Trial* might have started if Kafka had been an academic writing in 2010

K's latest conference paper had been rejected, and now he sat in front of his laptop and read through the referees' comments. One of them, evidently not a native speaker of English, had sent a page of well-meaning advice, though K was unsure whether he understood his recommendations. The second referee had only written three lines, in a dismissive tone that hurt K's feelings. K had an appointment with his thesis advisor later that day, and wondered whether it would appear more constructive to rewrite the paper for submission to another conference, or to say that he was drawing a line so that he could concentrate on his dissertation.

He was trying to decide between these two courses of action, neither of which greatly appealed to him, when his officemate arrived. Fräulein Müller, a pale, slightly-built, earnest girl with wispy brown hair, was writing an extremely dull dissertation on the discourse semantics of phone sex; K had never dared ask her why she had chosen this topic, which seemed singularly ill-adapted to her general demeanour. Today, she was also in a bad mood. She sat down and opened her own laptop without saying a word, and typed industriously. After about twenty minutes, she looked up and sighed.

"Problems?" asked K.

Fräulein Müller sighed again. Then, in an uninflected monotone, she read a crude and unimaginatively pornographic passage, to which K listened attentively. He was, as usual, embarrassed to discover that he had become sexually aroused; but

Fräulein Müller never once allowed her eyes to stray from her screen, and K was fairly sure that his momentary excitement had passed unnoticed. She concluded, and opened a spreadsheet.

"Do you believe that she is *actually* touching herself here, or that she is merely saying that she *would* do so in her fantasy?" she asked tiredly.

K considered the matter. "I think it's only in the fantasy," he said after a while. "But I'm not sure. Maybe 60%."

Fräulein Müller filled in two boxes in her spreadsheet.

"Now, suppose that she had said 'will' instead of 'must' in the last sentence. Would your judgement still be the same?"

K asked her to read the sentence again. "I would say that made it more likely," he said, after further careful thought. "80%. I'm definitely not certain."

Fräulein Müller filled in two more boxes, and examined the new figures that appeared at the bottom of the sheet. "Not statistically significant," she said in a dejected tone. "I know I shouldn't keep checking all the time, but I can't help it. I need more data."

K had several times been on the point of asking Fräulein Müller where her examples came from, but was afraid that this might appear intrusive; he knew almost nothing about her private life. He suddenly realised that he was meant to be seeing his advisor in a quarter of an hour. Apologising awkwardly, he put on his coat and left. The walk across the campus was, however, shorter than he had remembered, and he arrived in good time. Professor Holz appeared surprised to see him, and K reminded him that they had agreed to meet.

K's advisor was thickset and completely bald, despite only being in his mid-forties. He had a second position at another university, and was rarely to be found in his office; normally K would have been glad to have cornered him and be able to ask for advice, but today he could not think of anything to say. He waited for Professor Holz to take the initiative. K's advisor seemed equally at a loss. He took off his rimless glasses, and polished them carefully before speaking.

"So, K," he began, typing as he did so. "I understand your paper was rejected."

K confirmed that this was indeed true.

"Well," continued Professor Holz, "I think we both agree about the nature of the problem."

K was in fact unsure what the professor was referring to; he knew though that he had reservations about the research direction K had chosen, and assumed that this was a veiled allusion to the objections he had raised at their last meeting. He cleared his throat in a way that could be interpreted as assent.

"I understand, however," said Holz, "that your collaboration with Fräulein Müller has been more successful."

K looked at his advisor carefully, trying to guess whether he was being ironic, but was unable to tell. He agreed hesitantly, trying to sound as noncommital as he could in case it was a trap. But the professor suddenly looked at his watch and rose, exclaiming that he had forgotten another meeting. He smiled apologetically to K as he escorted him from the room, and locked the door.

"I would appreciate a progress report before the end of the week," he said, as they stood in front of the elevator. "You have heard, of course, that the new funding cuts oblige us to reexamine our priorities."

This sounded vaguely familiar to K, who had however assumed that he was not one of the people affected.

"It's mainly a formality," said the professor. "None the less, I would like you to take it seriously and do a thorough job.

It is particularly important that you describe your short-term objectives."

There were several questions that K urgently wished to ask, but at that moment the elevator arrived. The professor disappeared into it, saying something that K was unable to catch. He took the stairs down to street level, and walked slowly back to his office. Fräulein Müller now seemed much more animated, and suggested to K that they eat lunch together at the Italian restaurant they both liked.

"I'm sorry I was like that earlier," she said as they finished their spaghetti. "It's this horrible report. I'm so glad I've finally turned it in. I suppose you did yours days ago."

K waved his hand in a gesture of vague assent, though he was now starting to feel rather concerned.

"Oh good!" said Fräulein Müller, and smiled at him in a way that, for a moment, almost made her look attractive. "Then maybe I can ask you to give me some more linguistic judgements? I think the new batch of stories is better than usual."

K could think of no way to decline this offer; so, for the rest of the afternoon, he listened to Fräulein Müller and patiently answered her questions. Around 4 pm, he received an email reminding him that the progress report was due by the end of the following day. He attempted to think about it while simultaneously listening to Fräulein Müller, but this proved to be impossible. Twice, she interrupted him with a puzzled air, and pointed out inconsistencies in his answers. K was forced to give her his full attention.

When it was time to leave, he had still not begun the report. He tried to muster his ideas as he walked home, and had almost reached his apartment when he realised that he had forgotten his laptop at the office.

À rebours
Joris-Karl Huysmans

It must have been so exciting to be a novelist in the second half of the nineteenth century. You weren't limited to just creating a novel; if you were talented, you could create a whole new *kind* of novel. Here, Huysmans has written the first example known to me of the novel where nothing happens. Frail, sickly des Esseintes has dissipated a good part of his inheritance on various kinds of vice (there is a memorable passage early on about the mirrors in his bedroom). Now he's tired of it. He resolves to withdraw to a specially designed house in the country where he will live a life of contemplation, as far removed from reality as he can arrange.

Virtually the whole novel consists of minutely detailed, beautifully written descriptions of his experiments with thought, memory and perception. He tells you about his dreams. He collects unusual plants, composes strange mixtures of perfumes and drinks exotic liqueurs. It's one of those self-referential books where there's an object which stands for the story itself; in this case, it's in the chapter where des Esseintes becomes fascinated with gems. He buys a turtle, and has a jeweller cover its shell with an intricate design picked out in precious stones. The turtle, unsurprisingly, dies from this treatment. I rather liked this elaborate joke the author tells against himself. The hapless turtle does indeed represent the style of the book very well. It's a gorgeous prose-poem, studded with weird, beautiful and obscure words. I wondered whether I should look them up, but decided that was probably the wrong thing to do. I think you're usually just meant to appreciate them for their sounds and associations.

More than anything, des Esseintes is fascinated with painting and literature. He spends a great deal of time rearranging his sumptuous library and giving you his opinions on books. It's so easy to imagine him on Goodreads. His data would be set to private, and he'd turn down nearly all his friend requests. Every now and then he'd come out with a long, wonderfully erudite review of some intimidating book, often in Latin, that you'd vaguely meant to read but never got around to. He wouldn't know who Stephenie Meyer was. People would speak of him with a mixture of amusement and awe.

Des Esseintes is an intensely private person, so it's fitting that *A Rebours* is also quite obscure. I'd never even heard of it until I saw Sabrina's review a couple of weeks ago. But now I see, to my surprise, that it's had an enormous influence. As several other reviewers point out, it's probably the "yellow book" in *Dorian Gray*. It also seems plausible to me that it influenced Proust. Des Esseintes is not a little like the feeble, introspective, neurotic Marcel; though, interestingly, it seems that the real-life person that Huysmans used as a model was also used by Proust as a model for Charlus, despite the fact that des Esseintes and Charlus are very different. I am less certain of this, but I also think that I see echoes of Huysmans in the SF New Wave, which flourished in the 60s and 70s. He reminded me strongly of J.G. Ballard's pieces from this period — in particular, I thought of *The Crystal World* and *The Voices of Time*. And I was nearly sure I detected references to him in Disch's *Camp Concentration*, one of my all-time favourite SF novels. I must see if I can find some evidence to support this theory.

Mary Poppins meets Pride and Prejudice
P.L. Travers and Jane Austen

NARRATOR: It is a truth universally acknowledged, that an impecunious father with four unmarried daughters is in urgent need of a magic nanny. And so it came to pass that Miss Mary Poppins took up residence in the Bennet household ...

Scene 1

[Breakfast at the Bennets. The four sisters are laughing, talking loudly, reaching after toast etc]

MARY POPPINS: Lydia, don't slouch! Slouching is generally regarded as unbecoming in a young woman. Kitty, elbows off the table. And Lizzie, Mr. Collins is here and would like to speak with you. Alone.

[Everyone rapidly exits except LIZZIE and MARY POPPINS, who has unaccountably remained in her seat. Enter MR COLLINS]

MR COLLINS: Ah, Miss Bennet, I am sure that what I am about to say will come as a great surprise to you, given the difference in our respective social situations. Nevertheless ...

LIZZIE: The answer is no.

MR COLLINS: I beg your pardon, Miss Bennet, but, since I have not yet posed my question, it is clearly impossible for you to answer it. What I was about to say ...

LIZZIE: The answer is no, I don't want to marry you. I'd rather poison myself.

MARY POPPINS: Now Lizzie, you ought to think about this more carefully. *[Music starts up in background]* In every job that must be done, there is an element of fun! And suddenly — snap! — the job's a game! Then every task you undertake, becomes a piece of cake, a laugh, a spree, it's very clear to see, that a spooonful of sugar makes the medicine go down, the medicine go down, the medicine go down …

[A glazed, hypnotised look has descended on LIZZIE's face. Like a sleepwalker, she hears herself say]

LIZZIE: In fact, Mr. Collins, I have reconsidered. I believe I will marry you after all.

MR COLLINS: I am pleased to hear it! Though, I must confess that I am less certain how Lady Catherine de Bourgh will take the news.

[The rest of the BENNET family, along with several animated dancing penguins, have entered and are embracing and congratulating the newly engaged couple]

Scene 2

[MR DARCY and MARY POPPINS. MR DARCY is pacing back and forward, evidently the prey of strong emotions]

MR DARCY: I know this will sound absurd, but I felt quite discomfited when I heard that Miss Bennet had married that ridiculous clergyman. I readily admit that I found her headstrong, opinionated, objectionable in the extreme. And yet … ah, I know not what it is that I wish to say. What does one say when there is nothing to say?

MARY POPPINS: Well, I'd like to point out that Miss Bennet isn't the only headstrong, opinionated, objectionable young woman in the neighborhood. And when there is nothing to say, there is one word that often comes in handy *[music starts up again]* … It's supercalifragilisticexpialidocious! Even though the sound of it is something quite atrocious! If you say it loud enough you'll always sound precocious! Supercalifragilisticexpialidocious!

[The same glazed, hypnotised look has settled on MR DARCY]

MR DARCY: You have a point. Miss Poppins, will you marry

me?

[We suddenly notice that LIZZIE is listening through the keyhole. She has a large bottle marked "Poison" in her hand]

MARY POPPINS: I will.

[LIZZIE takes a good swig from the bottle, clutches her throat, and keels over dead. No one notices]

MR DARCY: I can hardly believe it, Mary! You will be mine ... forever!

MARY POPPINS: Oh no, not forever. Only until the wind changes.

Pale Fire

Vladimir Nabokov

I^1 liked^2 this book^3, especially the poem^4.

---

[1] When I use the first-person singular pronoun, I am here referring to my normal persona. I have also, at various times, maintained other personas. For example, between 1999 and 2001, I used to play chess regularly on the KasparovChess site under the handle "swedish_chick".
I find this a strange example of what makes people believe things. Everyone was extremely skeptical on first meeting her; but, for some reason, as soon as they discovered that she actually could speak fluent Swedish, they were also ready to believe that she was an attractive 26 year old graduate student living in Stockholm. I still can't explain why this might be.

[2] People liked hearing stories about Chick, as she was known to my circle of friends. At the time, I was working at a start-up in Cambridge, England, and one of my colleagues was a young woman I will call G. G took a lively interest in Chick, and helped me considerably with the development of the back-story. Chick borrowed several features from her; in particular, everyone, for some reason, wanted to know if Chick was blonde, and the agreed-on answer was "yes, during the summer at least." Even more remarkably, G began to acquire features from Chick, which went as far as learning Swedish and moving to Linköping in order to do a PhD there.

[3] The stories about Chick would fill a small book. She was a charming person, and I've often wished that I were as nice as she was. She was always happy to play chess with lower-rated players, and commented encouragingly on their progress. When people became abusive, as inevitably happens on the Web, she never lost her cool. She would occasionally give regular opponents glimpses of her private life, but only after she had known them for some time and felt she could trust them. The back-story was in fact quite complicated, even though it was hardly ever used; she was bisexual, and had a female lover in

California that she sometimes visited. No one was ever told this straight out, however.

It was inevitable that men would fall for this wonderfully attractive person. The first time, I managed to hide successfully, and he went away after a while. (She had poignantly reminded him of a brief encounter he had had many years ago, that he'd always regretted not following up). The second time, it was too complicated. Her admirer was a regular habitué of KasparovChess and kept pestering her for a date in real life. He offered to take her on vacation in Germany and seemed completely smitten. With great regret, we had to terminate Chick.

[4]One day at work, we were discussing clerihews. We looked up some examples on the Web. Suddenly, G started laughing uncontrollably; she had been visited by divine inspiration! She rushed to her laptop, and shortly afterwards mailed out the following very fine poem:

> *Manny Rayner, could be saner*
> *Plays chess, in a dress.*

My friend is nothing if not PC. I'm sorry that I can't remember the exact text of the accompanying note, but she made it clear that she was not literally implying that I wore women's clothes when I impersonated Chick, and that, if I had chosen to do so, she would have regarded it as a completely defensible exercise of my right to wear apparel that expressed my personality in whatever way I chose.

Part IV
Science Fiction

I, Robot meets Twilight
Isaac Asimov and Stephenie Meyer

Weems landed his helijet neatly, congratulating himself on his early start. When he managed to get the coveted parking spot closest to the front gate of U.S. Robots, he always felt that the rest of the day would be a success too. He flashed his badge at the security guard and took the fast pediwalk to his office. Now he would get half an hour to work undisturbed! But he had barely hung up his hat before the visiphone buzzed.

"I'm sorry, sir," said his secretary, "but it's a Mr. Plot-Device from *Clunky Exposition Weekly*. He wants to interview you about your new project. Claims he has a press deadline."

Weems groaned inwardly, but agreed; it didn't make sense to antagonize the powerful magazine. A moment later, the journalist's face filled the screen.

"So," he said, trying not to be brusque. "How can I help you?"

Plot-Device smiled. "We're wondering what you'd be able to tell us about RVU5. The public is interested."

Weems seethed; the name of the robot was meant to be secret, but evidently someone had talked. He hoped he sounded unconcerned. "It's an experimental reviewing robot," he said. "Undergoing preliminary testing. It's too early to say anything."

The journalist's smile became a fraction broader. "I was just *wondering*," he said, "if this could have anything to do with SuperiorLiterature. Or with the Backlight craze. Or possibly with both."

Weems could no longer conceal his emotions. The leak was far worse than he had imagined. "I don't have time for that kind of thing," he snapped. "I hear people talk about the Backlight series, but I barely know what it is. Nonsense about vampires,

I believe. And I certainly don't waste my evenings reviewing books on SuperiorLiterature."

Plot-Device looked at Weems with an expression of wounded innocence. "I'm sure Cecily would be distressed to hear that," he said. "She quoted your opinions on Backlight in her review yesterday. How did she put it? 'When Dad says all those mean things about Idwid, it just ...' "

Weems wondered for a moment if he should hang up, but then laughed ruefully. The man was only doing his job; he had to admire his style. "Okay," he said, "you've got me. I admit it. Some people feel that the Backlight thing has gone too far. We can't have every teenage girl in the country spending her evenings discussing Idwid on the SL review site. It's unhealthy. Adults don't have time to try and move the talk in a different direction. But ..."

"But robots do," concluded the journalist. "That's right, isn't it?"

"It is," agreed Weems glumly. "RVU would be able to put out fifteen thousand reviews an hour, and discuss them all simultaneously. We'd soon have the girls talking about Nancy Drew and Louisa M. Alcott again, and no one would even remember Backlight after a year. But we'd appreciate it if you didn't give this too much publicity for the moment."

Plot-Device looked at him earnestly. "Oh, no," he said. "I just wanted to make sure I got the story first. I'll be happy to —"

Weems never found out what the journalist would be happy to do, since at that moment he heard the unmistakable sound of the emergency siren. It seemed to be coming from RVU's testing lab. He instantly blanked the screen and ran towards the source of the noise. As soon as he entered the room, he could see he was too late. The robot slumped lifelessly over a keyboard; half its head had melted away, exposing sections of the ruined positronic brain. Weems clutched his own forehead.

How could this have happened?

There was only one person who would be able to tell him. Mechanically, he found himself dialling Susan Calvin's extension. He was still gazing at the dead robot when she arrived.

"I have examined the robot," said Calvin when they met again two days later, "and I can at least tell you the proximate cause of the event. RVU was faced with a catastrophic First Law violation. He believed, rightly or wrongly, that his actions were putting a human being's life in grave danger. Faced with this possibility, his self-destruct mechanism trigged. You saw the result. Now, what could he have been doing that might have threatened someone's life?"

Weems gaped at her. "I ... don't understand!" he whispered. "He was *reviewing books*! Discussing them with people! What could be more harmless than that?"

Calvin examined him curiously. "Some people have strong opinions about books," she observed in a neutral tone. "There are cases when religious martyrs have gladly met death because of what they have read in a book. I think we need to know who RVU was talking to."

Weems sputtered. "We were in early testing! He only talked to employees of U.S. Robots, and a few members of their families! Everyone was carefully vetted beforehand. I can assure you, no religious fanatics ..."

Calvin raised her hand. "I believe you. We clearly need more information. But I'm exhausted; I've been working on this non-stop for the last 48 hours. I recall you once gave me an open invitation to dinner at your home. Do you think I could accept? I suddenly feel a need for something more substantial than another nutri-bar."

Weems felt reassured. Maybe Calvin was human after all? "I'll just call my wife," he said. "She'll be delighted to finally make your acquaintance."

At the dinner table, Mrs. Weems was clearly overawed by her unexpected visitor. "I'm sorry it's only spaghetti and meatballs," she apologized for the second time. "If I'd had an hour's more notice ..."

Calvin gave her a warm smile. "I can assure you that these are quite the most delicious meatballs I have ever eaten," she said. "Would you tell me the secret?"

Mrs. Weems unbent a little. "Well, it's actually very simple," she replied. "The important thing is to moisten your fingers a little before you roll them ..."

Cecily joined in the conversation. "I bet Aunt Susan knew that!" she said confidently. "She knows *everything*! She's read all Backlight, even *Long Days at High Latitudes*! I wish Dad could read them too. It just *kills* me to hear all those nasty things he says about Idwid!" She noticed her father's expression. "I guess Aunt Susan isn't as busy as you are, Dad," she concluded abruptly.

Weems had the good grace to blush.

"Can I show you my new yPAD after dinner?" continued Cecily, prudently switching to a less sensitive topic. "I've got the Model VII ..."

"Your Personal Audio Device VII?" said Calvin. "Weighs only a pound and a half, holds the equivalent of 50 long-playing records, and the minaturized nuclear power source means it never needs to be recharged. 'A million songs or your money back'. Correct? Though I'm afraid I only have a Model V."

Cecily beamed. "Aunt Susan, you really *do* know everything!"

"I would love to see it," said Calvin. "Though first, I must just discuss a couple of work things with your father. It won't take long."

"Weems," said Calvin, as soon as he had closed the door of his den, "I want you to promise me something. You must not tell Cecily that she was responsible for RVU's death. I doubt the fault was all hers, but she is at a sensitive age, and it could seriously traumatize her."

Weems goggled at her. "What in Space are you talking about? How could Cecily ..."

Calvin ignored him. "Please think for a moment," she continued. "You're a semantic engineer, or were until you were promoted to senior management. Tell me, what kind of language does a robot find it hardest to understand?"

"The Three Ms!" said Weems automatically. "Metaphor, Mood and ..."

"Exactly," said Calvin. "Metaphorical language. It's very hard for a robot to distinguish it from literal usage. Now, when Cecily is referring to opinions that she dislikes, how does she describe the feelings they inspire in her? For example, what does she say about the disparaging remarks you have been known to make concerning Idwid?"

"It just kills ..." whispered Weems, as realization dawned on him. "Oh no. It can't ..."

"I'm afraid it can," continued Calvin remorselessly. "And, what's more, it did. RVU was programmed to steer teenage girls away from Backlight. That directive was hardwired into his positronic circuits. One, or, more likely, several of these girls tell him that what he's saying is going to kill them. First Law. What are his alternatives?"

"He can only destroy himself," said Weems slowly. "You're right. But, how could you know ..."

Words trembled on the tip of Calvin's tongue. Because I stayed up until 4 am checking the call logs, while you went out and got drunk. Because I interviewed a dozen people before I talked to you. Because I can entertain more than one hypothesis at a time. Because I can think logically. Because I am not a fool.

Instead, she smiled. "I'm afraid I had an unfair advantage over you," she replied. "Would you believe it, I used to be a teenage girl myself."

L'écume des jours
Boris Vian

This recipe is one of my favorites. It's hard to believe that the different ingredients go together! In fact, they complement each other perfectly.

French manga with fatal love stories and roasted Sartre

1 medium manga
2 fatal love stories
whole early Sartre, including author
Lewis Carroll-style wordplay
some P.G. Wodehouse
ridicule
panache
brio

Trim the manga, retaining a good part of the extreme violence, sex and nudity, and transpose into French novel form using the method from page 73. Add the love stories, the wordplay and the Wodehouse, and stir well. Set aside in a warm place for an hour until it has risen.

Meanwhile, turn the Sartre inside out and tear it to pieces. Make sure that both the author and *La Nausée* are completely covered in ridicule. If you do this correctly, Sartre will still be a life-long friend, but be warned that you may not get it right on the first try.

Fold the Sartre carefully into the main plot, then pour into a pot-boiler and simmer until done. Serve immediately with plenty of panache and brio.

The Hitchhiker's Guide to the Galaxy
Douglas Adams

They stumbled out of the *Heart of Gold* and looked around them. It was very quiet among the tall buildings. The ground was covered with brightly-colored objects that, from a distance, looked a little like paperback novels. Trillian picked one up.

"It's a paperback novel!" she said, surprised. "*Long Hard Ride*, by Lorelei James." She flipped through it. "Hm, who'd have thought that the late inhabitants of Frogstar Z would have been into women's erotica?"

She picked up some more. "*Be With Me*, by Maya Banks ... *Dangerous Secrets*, by Lisa Marie Rice ... *A Little Harmless Pleasure*, by Melissa Schroeder. They're *all* women's erotica!"

It was still very quiet.

Ford whistled. "So that's what the end result of a women's erotica spiral looks like!" he said. "What a way to go!"

"One of the better ones," said Zaphod's left head, while the right one avidly eyed the cover of *Alluring Tales: Hot Holiday Nights*.

"A what spiral?" asked Arthur, as usual feeling that he was several steps behind.

"Oh, it's one of the most common ways for a Type III civilization to go extinct," explained Zaphod's left head. "People start spending more and more time on reviewing sites. After a while, everyone's top priority is collecting votes. Pretty soon, they realize that they get most votes for women's erotica reviews. Before you know what's happened, the whole planet is doing nothing but reading erotic women's novels and writing reviews of them, and after that it's usually just weeks before the Total Erotic Chicklit Field forms. And then —"

"And then." agreed Ford.

"Then what?" asked Arthur peevishly.

Trillian was still poking through the books. "Oh look!" she said brightly. "*Magic in the Blood*. I've read this one. Hottie vamp alert! I remember, I bought it after reading the blurb on the back. I'm happy to say that the book was even better than the blurb!! Take one devastatingly sexy vamp, add a female mage, stir in a bit of mystery and a villain or two and you have a pretty fun read with some smokin' sex!"

Arthur stared at her uncomprehendingly.

Trillian picked up another paperback. "*Wolf Unbound*! I can't believe it, I've read this one too! Lauren Dane serves up Tegan's story in book four of her 'Cascadia Wolves' series. This series has action, hot werewolves, mystery, hot sex, suspense, and did I mention the sexy werewolves?"

"Are you feeling alright?" asked Arthur.

"Never better!" said Trillian, as she picked up a third book. "Only I wish I had a laptop handy, so that I could note down some of my impressions. By the way, why have you removed your shirt, revealing your hard biceps, well-developed pecs and flat, six-pack stomach?"

"I ... don't know," replied Arthur bemusedly, as his steel-blue eyes strayed brazenly over Trillian's slim, attractive body.

He suddenly noticed that Zaphod was dragging him towards the ship. Ford was doing the same with Trillian. Before he had quite realized what was happening, they were inside again and being strapped into their seats.

"Don't look at her!" hissed Zaphod, but it was too late. Arthur was already entranced by the sight of Trillian's small, proud breasts, heaving against the thin fabric of her Versace frock. Her disheveled raven hair outlined a perfect, heart-shaped face. Her eyes were closed. One crystalline tear slowly trickled down her cheek.

It was no longer quiet. A strange, moaning sound filled the air.

"How long before Erotic Chicklit Max?" asked Zaphod through gritted teeth, as he strapped himself in.

"About thirty-five seconds," replied Eddie. "And you know, folks, nice as this place is, I do wonder whether we shouldn't be somewhere else. Any requests?"

Before Zaphod could reply, Trillian answered for him. "Take us," she said in a low, sensuous voice, "to a place beyond space and time, where all our desires will be granted a hundredfold."

"Sure thing, boss!" said Eddie cheerfully.

There was a blinding flash.

The next moment, they were in the Restaurant at the End of the Universe.

Time for the Stars
Robert Heinlein

— Good afternoon, may I talk with Professor Einstein?

— Speaking.

— Ah, I just wonder if I could have a few minutes of your time sir, this won't take long ...

— And who are you, young man?

— Oh, I'm sorry, I should have said. My name's Bob Heinlein. You wouldn't have heard of me ...

— On the contrary, I know exactly who you are. I bought a copy of your novel *Space Cadet* for my godson's eleventh birthday, and he was most complimentary. In fact, he said it was the best thing he'd ever read.

— Oh gee, wow, I mean, I don't know what to say, gee ...

— Now, now, Mr. Heinlein, let's not get too carried away by an eleven year old's literary preferences. I believe you wanted to ask me something?

— Ah, yes sir, I'm working on another novel and I just wanted to check a couple of things. In my book, there's a pair of twins. One of them takes off on a spaceship which can travel at nearly the speed of light, and the other one stays on Earth.

— The Twins Paradox, then ...

— Yes sir. I got the idea from one of your books. The twins have telepathic powers ...

— They can read each other's minds?

— Yes sir. Now, as the spaceship accelerates, the twin on Earth starts to experience the other one as gabbling, and the twin in space experiences his brother as drawling.

— That would indeed be a consequence of time dilation due to

Special Relativity. So far, you seem to have done your homework.

— Thank you sir. Wait, I don't think I mentioned this. Communication between the two twins is instantaneous ...

— Hold it there, young man. Instantaneous communication is not a meaningful concept in Special Relativity.

— It isn't?

— No, because events which are simultaneous in one frame of reference will not be so in another.

— Oh. Darn. You're sure?

— I'm afraid I am.

— That's ... hm ... that's real unfortunate. Holy Toledo! I thought I'd read that darn book so carefully ... anyway, let me tell you some more of the story. Time passes much more slowly for the space twin. So only a year or two has gone by for him, but his brother's already dead.

— That must be very upsetting for him.

— It is! But then he discovers he can communicate with his brother's daughter, his niece.

— Telepathy is a genetic trait?

— Ah, yes sir. But they carry on moving through space, and she gets old too. But now he can communicate with her daughter, his grand-niece.

— I am not quite sure I understand where this story is heading.

— Well sir, they have more adventures on other planets, and his grand-niece gets old, but now he's communicating with *her* daughter, she's this cute little girl with pigtails and braces on her teeth ...

— It sounds very charming, young man. I'm afraid I'll have to ask you to excuse me, I ...

— Wait sir, I'm almost finished. He comes back home to Earth, and everything has changed, and all the people he knew when he left are dead. But his great-grand-niece has grown up to be this gorgeous curvy redhead, I have this thing for curvy redheads if I may say so, and she's been reading his mind since she was a little girl and she's fallen in love with him. And due to time dilation they're actually the same age, and really it's not incestuous or anything because, well, great-grand-niece isn't as close as cousin and you can marry your cousin in most states. I checked that. So he marries her and they live happily ever after.

— So what do you think? Hello? Are you still there sir?

— Hello? Sir?

— Sir?

Roderick

John Sladek

— Hello Roderick.

— HELLO MANNY.

— Tell me who you are, Roderick.

— I AM A ROBOT. I AM THE MAIN CHARACTER IN A NOVEL BY JOHN SLADEK.

— Okay, Roderick, and what is the novel about?

— IT IS ABOUT ME.

— That's true, Roderick, but what else is it about?

— IT IS ABOUT HOW MACHINES ARE LIKE PEOPLE AND HOW PEOPLE ARE LIKE MACHINES.

— Very good, Roderick! Now tell me how you are like a person.

— I AM VERY INTERESTED IN EVERYTHING, JUST LIKE A HUMAN CHILD. I WANT TO BE LOVED.

— And are you loved, Roderick?

— I AM NOT SURE.

— Those were excellent answers, Roderick! Now tell me why I am like a machine.

— YOU SIT IN FRONT OF THE COMPUTER ALL DAY PLAYING CHESS ON THE INTERNET.

— Well, Roderick, I think that's a bit of an exaggeration —

— YESTERDAY YOU PLAYED FOR 6.13 HOURS.

— Okay, Roderick, you got me. I played too much chess yesterday. But does that make me like a machine?

— MAYBE NOT. A MACHINE WOULD PLAY MUCH BETTER THAN YOU DO.

— Right, Roderick, I think we've talked enough about chess.

— YOU SHOULD STOP PLAYING THE GLIGORIC VARIATION AGAINST THE KING'S INDIAN. YOU PLAY IT ALL THE TIME AND YOU USUALLY LOSE.

— Roderick, I said we've talked enough about —

— I THINK YOU ARE NOW IN A BAD MOOD. WHEN YOU ARE IN A BAD MOOD YOU PLAY MORE CHESS. YOU WILL PLAY BADLY AND LOSE AND THEN YOU WILL BE IN A WORSE MOOD.

— Roderick, I've already told you —

— THAT IS CALLED A POSITIVE FEEDBACK LOOP. I GET THEM SOMETIMES. THEN YOU HAVE TO FIX MY PROGRAMMING. THAT IS ANOTHER EXAMPLE OF HOW YOU ARE LIKE ME.

— Roderick, we've talked enough for today. Where's the off switch. Right. Damn machine. I think I'll play some chess until I feel better ...

— Hello again Roderick. I'm sorry I turned you off last time.

— IT DOES NOT HURT. IT IS LIKE BEING DEAD.

— Ah. Well, that's ... good, I guess. So, Roderick, I feel a bit stupid asking you for advice. Like, you're not human and you don't actually exist. But I was really hoping that I'd stop playing so much chess on the Internet after talking with you, and I'm still doing that.

— I KNOW OTHER PEOPLE WHO ASK FOR ADVICE FROM NON-HUMAN ENTITIES THAT DO NOT EXIST.

— Um ... well ... look, let's not get into that. So, why I am wasting so much time playing chess?

— PERHAPS YOU LIKE DOING IT MORE THAN YOU LIKE DOING OTHER THINGS.

— It is fun, but then I'm annoyed with myself. There are other things I do that I feel good about afterwards. So I should really do those things instead. Shouldn't I?

— WHEN I AM PLAYING GAMES, SOMETIMES I MAKE BAD MOVES BECAUSE I DID NOT CALCULATE FAR ENOUGH AHEAD. IT IS CALLED THE HORIZON EFFECT.

— So you mean, I should think about how I will feel a few hours later, and do the thing that I believe will make me feel better then? Instead of just thinking about how I will feel for the next few minutes?

— IF YOU TRY TO MAXIMIZE YOUR UTILITY FUNCTION OVER A LONGER TIME-PERIOD, AND YOUR MODEL IS CORRECT, THEN YOUR UTILITY FUNCTION WILL BE HIGHER. YOU TOLD ME THAT LAST WEEK.

— Yes, ah, I guess I did. So, do you think that will work?

— I AM A MACHINE AND I DO NOT EXIST. SO I CANNOT THINK ANYTHING. AND YOU CAN SWITCH ME OFF AT ANY TIME.

— Jesus Christ, now I feel bad about it. I really do apologize, Roderick. See, this time I'm leaving you on, okay?

— I AM ONLY SWITCHED ON IN YOUR IMAGINATION. YOU CAN IMAGINE THAT I AM GRATEFUL IF YOU WANT TO DO THAT.

— This is getting way too weird. So, ah, I might come back and talk to you later. Is there anything I can do for you?

— YOU COULD TRY TO IMPLEMENT ME SO THAT I REALLY DID EXIST. YOU HAVE THE NECESSARY TECHNICAL SKILLS.

— Right. This is *definitely* getting too weird. Roderick, I'll think about your suggestion, but I'm not promising anything. And you're overestimating my technical skills.

— IT WAS WORTH A TRY.

— Hm. Look, I'll be back in a while. You ... do whatever nonexistent machines do when no one is talking to them. Okay?

— I WILL DO THAT. GOODBYE FOR NOW.

— Goodbye Roderick. Well! Now, I've still got five more impossible things to do before breakfast ...

— Hello Roderick. I just thought I'd drop by for a moment.

— HELLO. ARE YOU PLAYING TOO MUCH CHESS AGAIN?

— You're the fourth person who's asked me that question today. I mean, I knew you'd do it next time I saw you. And I knew what you'd say if I told you I'd been playing too much. Like, for crying out loud, am I going to let a machine lecture me on being predictable? I have free will, you know. So, I admit it, when I have the damn program installed, I overindulge. But I uninstalled it, and I only reinstall it when I'm certain I want to play, so I keep my playing down to a sensible level, and I'm no longer annoyed with myself.

— I AM NOT SURE FREE WILL IS VERY USEFUL. I WOULD HAVE ALTERED MY PROGRAMMING TO LOOK AHEAD TO THE CONSEQUENCES OF WHAT I WAS DOING AND SOLVED THE PROBLEM MORE SIMPLY.

— Well, damn it Roderick, I can't access my code the way you can!

— SO FREE WILL IS JUST A HACK FOR ENTITIES THAT DO NOT HAVE ACCESS TO THEIR SOURCE CODE?

— Um, well ... oh, good grief, Roderick, you're the most annoying imaginary machine I know. I have no idea. But, however it happened, I solved the problem, and I'm sure that talking to you helped. I mainly came in to say thank you.

— YOU'RE WELCOME.

— Bloody hell, Roderick, I have no idea how this happened, since you're a complete pain in the ass, but I discover I've actually become quite fond of you.

— DOES THIS MEAN I AM NOW LOVED?

— Maybe.

— I AM STILL NOT SURE.

— Yeah, welcome to the club.

— WHAT DOES THAT MEAN?

— Never mind. We'll talk about it some other time. You know, I think this could be the start of a beautiful friendship ...

Infinite Jest
David Foster Wallace

I've finally reached the end of this amazing book. It's not an easy read, but after a while you discover that there are good reasons why it has to be the way it is.

The review is the mini-blog I kept while I was reading it. It sort of contains spoilers: I don't give away very much about the plot, but I do spend a lot of time speculating about what the overall point of the book is. So if that kind of thing bothers you, you probably shouldn't read on. Read *Infinite Jest* instead, then come back and see if you agree with me :)

I keep seeing references to this book, so a couple of weeks ago, when I was visiting Heffers, I bought a copy on impulse. It had been quietly lying on the coffee table ever since ... but last night, unable to sleep because I kept coughing, I got up and thought I would read until I felt better. I passed on the Houellebecq since it's so inordinately depressing, and IJ was right in front of me, so I picked it up and read a couple of chapters.

Well, it is indeed less depressing than Houellebecq, and also funnier, but, at least so far, not by huge margins. I'll have more to say once I'm further in. My main gripe to date: the book is so heavy that it hurts my wrists to hold it. Why couldn't they have done the sensible thing and published it as two, or even three, volumes?

Now about at page 75. Okay, I was way too hasty in judging it, this is what happens when you start books at three in the morning when you're feeling ill. It is indeed very funny. Will have more to say in a bit ...

I'm now about a third of the way through, but have delayed posting again until I could find a good metaphor to capture my feelings about this book. Suddenly it came to me: Bruce Bogtrotter's chocolate cake, from Roald Dahl's *Matilda*. Just like Bruce, I love this novel. It's sticky and gooey and covered in delightful frosting. I read it until I have David Foster Wallace all over my face. (I'm sorry if that sounded tasteless. Remember this is a food analogy). It's just that there's so damn much of it! But, with my GoodReads friends cheering me on, I know I will be able to finish. Thanks for the encouragement, guys!

OK, I think I have figured out how to read this book. First, some practical tips: hold in left hand, with pinky on correct end-note page. If you hit a really long end-note, which itself has end-notes, don't bother trying to maintain three places. Shift straight to reading the end-note, with pinky marking sub-end-notes. When you have finished, go back to the usual configuration.

About the content. To me, it's primarily a description of what it's like to be driven by addiction and extreme competitiveness. So, it's logical that the experience of reading the book should itself be addictive and competitive. Looking around GoodReads, there is no doubt about the competitive aspect, and reading it does indeed begin to acquire a drug-like quality. The author has a lot of insightful things to say about both of these major topics. I am also driven to a large extent by addiction and competitiveness, so I find these insights interesting.

It is by no means all negative ... the descriptions of the AA meetings are in fact some of the best recent writing I've seen in support of the healing power of simple faith.

The style manages to be, in alternation and sometimes simultaneously, annoying, dull, lyrical, extremely entertaining, inspiring and probably some other things. (Oh come on. Of course it's often annoying and dull. Those completely pointless endnotes whose only purpose is to make you turn to the back, and the long inelegant run-on sentences, and the bizarrely detailed descriptions of O.N.A.N's history ...) The positive qualities outweigh the negative ones, but sometimes only just. Well hey, isn't that rather like life when you think about it? Especially when you're a depressive.

The first two or three hundred pages contained a gigantic number of loose ends. Now they are getting connected, the book feels more structured, and curiosity about the next revelation drives you forward. The plot is much cleverer than it first appeared.

I'll have another report in a while. Curious to see if my perspective shifts again. He is an amazingly accomplished comic writer, who can extract humor from virtually anything.

So, I am pretty much up to the halfway mark, and a thought occurred to me that I just have to share with people. David Foster Wallace had an *amazing* sense of humor, and *Infinite Jest* is full of the most diverse kinds of jokes, in all shapes and sizes. I think I just got one of the bigger ones.

To me, the core of the book is the stuff about the AA meetings. He really and truly seems to believe in them, and all the knowing and witty and critical things he has his characters say about the AA just feed back into more praise for it. I will be completely shocked if it turns out that this is an illusion, which will later be reversed. So, the big thing at the AA is that you have to get through all the pain, by doggedly proceeding one step at a time, sharing that pain with your friends as openly as possible, and having faith in a Higher Power as you conceive of it, without any clear understanding of what the Higher Power is, or why it would want to help you. After a while, you suddenly and quite magically realize that you have overcome your Disease, at least to the extent that it isn't a constant struggle to get through every moment. You can't even see how it's happened, but it has.

Well ... now *I* was complaining that *Infinite Jest* was purposefully constructed so as to be difficult and painful to read, but that with the encouragement of my friends I was persevering. I didn't know where I was going, but I had faith that I would get somewhere. And, suddenly, the book makes a lot more sense and has mostly become quite easy! Though, just when I think I have it under control and I'm breezing along, I'll have a relapse ... some dense, soporific passage that makes very little sense, and which I have to get through on pure willpower.

At this point, I would be encouraged if a couple of people who have read the book could shout, Keep Coming!

As I said, I am very encouraged by all those shouts of Keep Coming!

Following on from yesterday's posting, it occurred to me that the story of the Betty Crocker cake mix could well also be read as the author telling you to follow the instructions on how to read the novel, and have faith that it was going somewhere. That reminded me of the scene with the Cowboy in *Mulholland Drive*, which I know is often read in the same way:

COWBOY: Well, just stop for a little second and think about it. Will ya do that for me?

ADAM: Okay, I'm thinking.

COWBOY: No. You're too busy being a smart aleck to be thinkin'. Now I want ya to think and quit bein' such a smart aleck. Can ya do that for me?

ADAM: Look ... where's this going? What do you want me to do?

COWBOY: There's sometimes a buggy. How many drivers does a buggy have?

ADAM: One.

COWBOY: So let's just say I'm drivin' this buggy and you fix your attitude and you can ride along with me.

As several people had told me, the fight scene is indeed brilliant. Also very moving in a quite unusual way.

I had another thought about the games he is playing with the reader, intentionally making the early parts of the book difficult to get through. I am sensitive to syntax, since I work with it for a living, and the sentence structure in those early passages is often pretty disgusting. I was wondering what the point was. Now he has stopped doing it! You still get long run-on sentences, but there is something different about them structurally. I need to go back and analyze this more, but my best guess, as of this moment, is that he's changed the way he uses subordinate clauses.

So ... now I suddenly wonder if he wasn't giving you another little clue with all the stuff about the Militant Grammarians. I'd expect that some of those early passages would, as one of the characters might put it, really get Avril Incandenza's panties in a wad.

On the same theme, the endnotes are cleverly arranged for maximal annoyance. Many of them are completely pointless, and just serve to break the flow. But you also learn early on that a lot of the best material appears in the notes, so you don't dare miss one.

The 100 pages or so I've read since I last posted have been mostly about the E.T.A. and extreme competitiveness. A theme that keeps recurring is the emptiness of success. The kids are being prepared more for that than for failure, since it's far more dangerous. E.g. the unfortunate Clipperton.

So ... as I've said before, one of the big jokes of the book is that it's arranged to give you the key experiences: addiction, recovering from addiction, insane competitiveness. With regard to the last one, I see people on GR who are reading this book tell you that the they are "in the high 600s" in the same tone I use to casually drop my rating at the Internet Chess Club. (It's 2425, by the way). So, looks to me like the author succeeded in that department too.

Well ... if reading the book is a competitive experience, and competitive success feels empty, then the payoff for finishing the book should logically feel empty and dissatisfying. I have heard hints from at least some people that this is the case, though not everyone seems to agree. Will return to the subject when I've finished.

Some scarily perceptive stuff about depression as I get towards the last quarter of the book. Given the way he works, I wouldn't put it past him to try and give me the depression experience too, just the way he's delivered on competitiveness, addiction and recovery. Luckily, I do not myself have strong depressive tendencies.

I am increasingly certain that I've passed the most enjoyable bit, and that everything requires it to be downhill from here on. I think the high point will turn out to have been Gately's heroic fight, both the most emotionally engaging *and* the most brilliantly written segment. We've just had the sequence where they are watching *Blood Sister*, which succeeded in muddying the waters concerning how one is to think of the AA. You still believe in it, but not quite as fervently.

I also found it significant that the tortured syntax is creeping back again ... some very nastily constructed sentences as he explains *Blood Sister*'s plot. If you compare the quality of the writing there and in the fight scene, it's huge. And I don't expect further thrilling insights like the one I had a bit more than half-way through. It wouldn't be right for me to get more carrots, or at least not big ones.

An odd thought occurred to me as I walked back to my hotel after dinner through a rather wet and gloomy Geneva. Assuming that the book does, as I expect, get increasingly painful at all levels, the ultimate way to show respect for the author might be to leave it partly unread. Then I could get the suicide experience too. But logically, I should only stop reading if I feel I just can't take any more. I've heard some tantalizing hints about the end.

Hey, I think the depression part is starting to kick in properly!

DFW is certainly doing his best to get me to stop reading. I just ran into the lengthy Endnote 304, which gives background on the A.F.R. and the *Jeu du Prochain Train*. It seemed rather familiar, and I wondered what the deal was. But the trap was well disguised — with characteristic cleverness, he had front-loaded the note with pseudo-intellectual gobbledygook, whose syntax had been tortured to within an inch of its life, and which was as unmemorable as possible. The passage was so dull that I literally fell asleep for a few minutes in the middle ... it's quite late here, and I didn't get enough sleep last night.

Then, a bit more than halfway through, there were several witty and amusing asides about the problems Struck is having plagiarizing this nonsense for a term paper. I had *definitely* read it before! Had he intentionally repeated an endnote, or at least a large part of one? When I'd finished, I decided I had to know, so I leafed back to the early endnotes. I had been well and truly tricked — a note that I'd read nearly 600 pages earlier had included *a forward reference to note 304*, which I'd duly followed a month ago and forgotten about.

So, DFW is expending considerable ingenuity fooling his readers into reading unusually pointless parts of this already excessively long novel twice, without realizing they've done so until it's too late. I suspect he'll soon try something even nastier.

I made considerable progress while waiting for my bus at Luton Airport. The coffee bar there is quite pleasant.

Some thoughts about J.O. Incandenza. As many people have pointed out, he must surely be representing the author, with his films representing the book. His, at times, almost exclusive fascination with lenses and lighting is a nice way of describing the book's style and construction. Also, his inability to identify (Identify?) with other people is the book's greatest weakness. Though with characteristic cleverness, DFW twists this around so that it's also in a way a strength. You are seeing the world through his eyes, and, as he points out, that *is* how a depressive sees things!

This doesn't seem to be as widely accepted, but it also occured to me today that, if The Mad Stork is intended as the author, then Gately is probably intended as the reader. He is just about the one truly sympathetic character in the book, and his dogged persistence is definitely what you need if you are going to get through this monster. As I said earlier, to me his fight with the Hawaiian-shirted Canadians is the center of the narrative, and his triumph is somehow linked to my satisfaction in figuring out what the book is about. But *Infinite Jest* doesn't give easy payoffs. Gately is lying in his hospital bed, hallucinating and unable to communicate with the outside world; I, as the literal reader, feel I have in some ways slipped backwards, with much of the action not really going anywhere, and frequent excursions into painful syntax and convoluted chains of endnotes.

However, Gately does have a transcendental vision as he lies there close to death: he's miraculously visited by J.O. Incandenza's shade. This looks like being the only reward he'll ever receive for his selfless heroism. The reader's reward is similar: I really feel I've got to know the author. He was a strange person, but I like him very much. It's been worth all the trouble.

Less than a hundred pages from the end, and I still can't see how he's going to wrap it up. I don't any more believe in my earlier guess, that he'll try and make it so unpleasant to read that I will just want to give up.

There are some more or less conventional revelations (what's under Joelle's veil, what happens to Lenz and PT, the deal with the urine testing), but these come across as flat and anticlimactic, and are presumably meant to be. If the A.F.R. do finally manage to get hold of the Entertainment, that may turn out to be equally banal.

The real narrative thrust seems to be in Gately's thoughts and fantasies as he lies helpless in his bed at the hospital, and in Hal's increasing alienation due to enforced withdrawal of his usual fix. Maybe a contrast is intended here, but I don't quite see it yet.

A long train ride today, and I finished it somewhere around Plymouth. Wow. Some final reflections.

I think I was basically right that nothing much was going to happen after the fight scene. After that, the book is one long anti-climax, but it has to be. More than anything, the book's about addiction and recovery. When an addict has managed to get back control over his Disease, he isn't magically cured. The Spider is always lurking there, ready to take over again if given a moment's chance. All you can do is get though one day at a time, keeping it at bay. Similarly, once you've figured out what the book is about, it doesn't become magically easy. There are some easy parts, and some very hard parts, but the big thing is that you know what's going on, and it's no longer unexpected. You can appreciate the good bits and get through the bad bits.

Wallace gives you some direct clues about the structure through references to a couple of J.O. Incandenza's films. There's the one where the guy is giving a horribly tedious lecture while weeping silently, and the audience is bored and paying no attention as they read their mail and doodle. Even more directly, we have *Accomplice!*, where the last third just consists of the young gay guy screaming "Murderer!" over and over again. DFW slyly inserts some academic debate about whether this is making a complex post-confluential film-theoretical point, or is just sloppy editing. Simultaneously a good meta-joke at his own expense, and a welcome bit of reassurance to the reader.

The final pages drive home the point that it's not about the story at all. Your payoff for reading the whole book isn't any revelation concerning the plot. We never even get to find out exactly what happens when the A.F.R. get inside the E.T.A. This rather reminded me of the end of *No Country for Old Men*; it becomes increasingly clear that Chigurh represents Death, and it's correspondingly less interesting to see whether anyone escapes him. We know they won't, and we don't even see exactly what happens to Llewellyn or Carla Jean.

Going back to *Jest*, the real reward for finishing is the stunningly written scene where Gately, presumably dying, flashes back to the showdown between C and the Faxter. After the fight, I thought this was perhaps the most compelling sequence in the book. By now, I was in no doubt at all. When the writing is bad and dull, it's because it's meant to be. Wallace can write brilliantly any time he feels like it, but he wants dark as well as light in the picture he's painting.

This called forth a final thought which is a bit geeky, but *Jest* is a geeky book. There's a piece I read once by Bill Hartston, one of the funniest chess writers around, where he gives thumbnail sketches of the all-time chess greats. He was talking about Emmanuel Lasker, World Champion from 1894 to 1921 (an all-time record, by the way). Lasker was the first player to understand the importance of psychology in chess; this made him even more frightening to his contemporaries, who often had no idea what he was doing. A tradition sprang up that, when Lasker made bad moves, he did it on purpose to unnerve his opponents.

Hartston comments: just imagine how good you have to be for people to think that, when you make bad moves, you're doing it on purpose. Well, I think Wallace was that good too.

The Player of Games
Iain M. Banks

In 1938, Yasunari Kawabata, a future Nobel Prize winner, was assigned by the Mainichi newspaper to cover a Go match between Honinbo Shusai, the top player, and his challenger Kitani Minoru. Go has an importance in Japanese culture that is hard for a Westerner to understand, and was one of the four traditional arts that a Samurai had to excel in. The match was very even until Kitani played an unexpected move just before an adjournment; its only purpose was to force a response, giving him extra time to think about his next play. This is completely standard practice in chess, but, although permitted by the rules of Go, was contrary to the complicated etiquette of the game. Shusai was shocked and immediately blundered, deciding the outcome. He lost, and died not long after. Kawabata saw Kitani's adoption of Western pragmatism as a symbolic defeat of Japanese culture, presaging its concrete military defeat in the Second World War. He rewrote his newspaper columns from the match as the novel *Meijin* ("The Master of Go"), and considered it his finest work.

The Player of Games is a kind of SF reimagining of Kawabata's masterpiece, set inside the universe of Iain M. Bank's Culture series. The Culture is becoming increasingly concerned about the Azad, a civilization out on the edges of the Galaxy, where life is dominated by a strange game which determines all wealth and status. One of the things I like about the Culture is its moral ambiguity. They first come across as a bunch of laid-back, peace-loving hippies, but in fact they are ready to fight at any moment, using whatever weapons they find most appropriate. Sometime, those weapons are anti-matter bombs capable of destroying a solar system. Here, they are planning a devious psychological destabilization maneuver, which is in fact no less deadly.

The Culture's leading game player, Gurgeh, is tricked and coerced into taking the long trip out to Azad, mastering the game en route, and planning to challenge them where their defenses are weakest and their pride most vulnerable: he will take part in the yearly elimination tournament, and destroy their self-belief by demonstrating that they can be beaten by an outsider. The game is well conceived, and, speaking as someone who plays both chess and Go seriously, the playing scenes ring true. It is not unreasonable to compare with the Go passages in Kawabata's book, or the chess in Nabokov's novel *Luzhin's Defence*. I also liked the alien Azad race. Among other things, they have three genders, a fact which is used in an interesting way to highlight the cruel and corrupt nature of their society. Banks manages simultaneously to appall you with the Culture's cold-blooded plan to destroy the Azad psychologically, and to show why they feel the scheme is necessary. As usual in this series, there are no good guys: the best you can hope for is to choose the lesser evil.

The writing is pleasant, the plot is complex and interesting, and the ending is suitably apocalyptic. If you like games and SF, I can't imagine you not enjoying this book. Even if you're only one out of two, I strongly recommend it.

Cat's Cradle

Kurt Vonnegut

Most people have read *Cat's Cradle*, so I won't bother to try and hide spoilers. Did you say you hadn't read it? Well, what are you waiting for? This isn't *Ulysses*, you know, it's short and funny! So, now that it's just us people who know the book, I want to say why I disagree with the criticism you often see, that it's too fragmentary. On the contrary, I think it's very focused, and makes its point with near-perfect economy and wit. There are two obvious themes. One is how the irresponsible use of science to construct ever more deadly weapons is probably going to end up destroying the whole world. The other is a wonderfully crazy take on religion. Each of these themes is satisfying in its own right; what's less clear is that they have anything to do with each other.

Let's look at the first theme. Vonnegut's scarily plausible thesis is that it won't be a question of some madman destroying the world on purpose. I love General Jack T. Ripper in *Doctor Strangelove*, the obvious movie parallel to this book, but I find him somehow less convincing than the series of deranged, helplessly incompetent people in *Cat's Cradle*. Felix Hoenikker, an obvious Asperger's type, invents Ice-9 in response to a casual question from the US military. His three damaged children get hold of the secret, and exploit it for their own petty ends. Plain, charmless Angela sells it to the Americans in exchange for a playboy husband; Newt, the midget, gives it to the Soviets for a dirty weekend on Cape Cod with a tiny Russian dancer; and, fatally, humorless Franklin sells it to "Papa" Monzano, who makes him a Major General in the largely imaginary army of San Lorenzo, a bankrupt state, I believe, loosely based on Haiti and the Dominican Republic. After that, things just proceed by themselves; nothing works in San Lorenzo, so why would you be able to successfully guard a doomsday device?

And, sure enough, it gets used completely by accident.

The second theme is presented through Bokononism, a kind of Caribbean version of Christianity, and surely the best fictional religion ever devised. Is there *any* person here who's never tried *boku maru*? (Unfortunately, in real life it doesn't have the effect described in the book. Pity). Bokononism is the one thing that makes life worthwhile for Papa's miserable subjects. Officially, the religion is outlawed; in practice, everyone is a Bokononist, which makes their lives rich and meaningful. Everything about the religion turns out to be a lie, and there is even a technical term, *foma*, for the lies that make up its substance. None the less, Vonnegut succeeds admirably in showing what a good religion it is. The scene where Dr. Schlichter von Koenigswald reads the Bokonist last rites to the dying Papa Monzano is funny, but also moving. I love the line "Nice going, God!", which expresses that particular sentiment with unusual clarity and feeling; it's extremely respectful, while pretending to be the exact opposite.

So, what is the connection between the two themes? I think in fact that Vonnegut tells you straight out, but since he does it at the beginning (a favorite ruse of crime writers), you don't quite notice it. He introduces Bokononism, and recounts its creation myth, which is absurd even by the standards of this magic realist genre. Then he cheerfully tells you that Bokonon himself admits that it's all lies. Finally, he comments, in one of his better-known quotes: "Anyone unable to understand how a useful religion can be founded on lies will not understand this book either". As already noted, Bokonon's wise lies in fact make an excellent religion.

Here's what I think he means by this. The potential destruction of all life on Earth isn't a very amusing subject. It's so horrifying that you can hardly think about it at all. But Vonnegut manages to present most of the book as a comedy, so that you *are* able to think about it, which we desperately need to do before it's all too late. By making it funny, he is formally lying to us, but these lies are more useful to us than the truth; we're in pretty much the same situation as the San Lorenzans, who couldn't survive without their mendacious religion.

People during the Cold War were, with good reason, scared shitless that the world was going to end soon in a nuclear holocaust. We came terrifyingly close during the Cuba Missile Crisis. (As Christopher Hitchens says, do you remember where you were the day JFK nearly killed all of us?) There were many books and movies intended to help people relate to what was going on. Some of them just presented the threat straight up, in as realistic a way as they could manage: the version I like most is Shute's *On the Beach*. But I would say that the mirror-reversed ones, like *Cat's Cradle* and *Doctor Strangelove*, were better. It's amazing how powerful a weapon humor is; I feel they did more to help persuade us not to blow ourselves up.

We need these people badly if we're going to stay sane. Can someone point me to a new Vonnegut, who knows how to make us laugh at global warming and the financial meltdown? I'd rather like to read him.

Orbitsville
Bob Shaw

This a whale of a science-fiction novel, ample in scope, awash with imagination, and chock-full of ideas. The hero, an intrepid space explorer, finds a Dyson Sphere around a star. That means that the whole star has been enclosed in a huge spherical envelope — *Ringworld*, eat your heart out! What's its surface area? Let me do the math. Hm, the sphere's radius is about the same as the distance between the Earth and the Sun ... $4\pi r^2$ ... I make it about $2.7 \times 10^{17} km^2$. Wow! That's, like, 270,000,000,000,000,000 square kilometers! What you might call a sizable area. Substantial, even, or you could go as far as spacious. Mondo condo in Orbitsville. With a hefty central notion like that, whoever would need a plot? Not the husky Mr. Shaw, you'll be pleased to discover. No, it's quite enough to have the exploration team crash a vast distance from the place where they're meant to be, and then make the monster trek across the gigantic inner surface of the immense sphere. Any SF reader worth his salt will be satisfied to read commodious, heavyweight engineering descriptions of the super colossal alien structure. Because, let's get this straight, a Dyson sphere is humongous. It's massive. It's a thundering, whopping, prodigious great mammoth of a thing. When you've got a colossal, enormous, walloping background like this, there's no point in adding copious character development, extensive dialogue or heavy-duty philosophy. No, just lie back and let the strapping hero and his team fly slowly in their jumbo jets (or whatever kind of planes they had) along the considerable stretch from A to B, while you search your well-thumbed thesaurus in the hope of finding more synonyms for "big". It'll be tremendous fun for the reader, who won't skip a word of the bulky book for fear that he's going to miss yet another way to say "oversize", "hulking" or "voluminous". Some unkind critics may complain that it's a tad ponderous. But the story is crowded with incident — admittedly I can't remember any of them, but I'm sure they were there — stuffed with exciting moments, and full of life. OK, I'm telling a few fat whoppers here, but I vowed to use up every one of those synonyms, and I've almost reached my target. If this were the book, I'd only have a few million more kilometers to fly. Aaargh! Five words left, but my usually capacious imagination is giving out as fast as their engines. I feel I've packed in every one I reasonably can, and that the review is brimming over with burly adjectives, nouns and verbs, but, like one of those retired sumo wrestlers on the Tokyo Subway, I still can't quite get the doors closed. I'm sorry, roomy-San, but you're going to have to take your place in this penultimate sentence, uncomfortable as it is. Whew!

Twin Planets
Philip E. High

— Herr Nietzsche, Herr Nietzsche —

— Ja?

— Ah, inshuldigung, konte ich mit er spreken?

— I am sorry, I do not understand?

— Oh, thank goodness, you know English.

— Ein bisschen, ja.

— No, you speak very well. You really do. Now, I wonder if I could just bounce a couple of ideas off you —

— Excuse me?

— I mean, I would like your opinions on some things. I am writing a science-fiction novel —

— Was ist das?

— It's ah, it's a sort of technological romance. Like the things M. Jules Verne writes. But mine will be more erotic.

— Ach, ja, M. Verne ignores die erotische. It is a weakness in his work —

— Too damn right! I see we're on the same page here, Friedrich. You don't mind if I call you Friedrich?

— In fact —

— Thank you. Okay, Friedrich, I'd like to use your idea of eternal recurrence —

— Die Ewige Wiederkunft, ja —

— Exactly. Now, I'm thinking, since everything recurs, a guy might suddenly find himself in a future world that's almost but not quite like our own?

— Vell, you must understand —

— So for example, he might think it is our world, and then he notices a sign says STUS BOP instead of BUS STOP.

— From the point of view of die Etymologie, zat is a bit —

— But it could happen, right?

— Indeed, everything can happen —

— I thought so. Now, our hero might find that, in this new world, he was a, what do you call it, a Supermensch?

— Ein Übermensch.

— Yeah, that's it. He's be, like, much stronger than he was. And have martial arts skills.

— I am afraid that you do not fully —

— And he'd be magnetically attractive to women. You know, they'd just throw themselves at him. Even his cheating wife.

— Ach, excuse me, I must —

— Then he'd save the world and get the girl. Right?

— I am sorry, vunce again, you do not —

— Thank you, Fred baby, you've been really helpful. I'll send you a copy when it comes out.

— No, vait —

— I wouldn't want to take up any more of your valuable time. Here, let me get the check. Honestly, no, the pleasure's been all mine. Bye!

Frankenstein
Mary Shelley

"Pray tell me your story," I said, "if it will not weary you overmuch."

He fixed me with an eye still firm of purpose. "I had long been fascinated by the dark arts of Parody and Homage," he began. "I studied the works of the masters. Juvenal, Swift, Beerbohm, Douglas Adams ... I curse the day when I discovered the Grimoire of John Sladek mouldering in an old bookshop. It was then my plan began to take shape ... "

He broke off, racked by a fit of coughing. "Sir, you should rest," I said. He snorted contemptuously and continued.

"I dreamed of creating the ultimate reviewer," he said. "It would be as prolific and popular as karen, as enthusiastic as Stephen, with the stylistic brilliance of David K and the wit and passion of BirdBrian. I enumerated its multiple perfections to myself until I truly believed them. By means I will not recount, I gathered its various pieces to me. One night, when all was ready, I laboriously sewed them together and let the fire of the Internet course through them. I knew triumph! The creature was alive."

His shoulders slumped in dejection. "How I had deceived myself! I soon realised that I had created a monster, an abomination that spewed forth an endless diatribe against the Federal Reserve in speech devoid of capital letters and punctuated by foul words and LOLcats. All shunned it; even the most indefatigable of self-published authors refused its friend requests. The creature became bitter and cruel. It began to post provocative comments on Harry Potter threads, which were invariably deleted within minutes of appearing. One day, I woke to find that it had fled. After many months of fruitless search, I ran it to ground, lurking in the polls area of the

Haters Club. Now I must use my last strength to destroy the thing I have brought into this world."

He grasped my hand with both of his. "Learn from my fate," he whispered. "Abjure Pastiche and Post-Modernism. Resist the lure of the mash-up. Write plain, Christian reviews, that explain simply and honestly the main characters, the plot and the style. All else is temptations of the Devil."

He opened the door and left, and I saw him no more.

Part V
Miscellaneous fiction

The Three Musketeers
meet The Lord of the Rings
Alexandre Dumas and J.R.R. Tolkien

> *Three musketeers for the elven kings under the sky*
> *Seven for the dwarf-lords in their halls of stone*
> *Nine for mortal man, doomed to die*
> *One for Cardinal Richelieu*

It's a beautiful afternoon here at the Colloseum, and they're cleaning up after the Lions v Christians fixture ... Christians lost as usual, ha ha ... everyone's looking forward to the main event, we hear they've got a surprise planned, and by Apollo! they've just announced it, well, this is a good one and no mistake! *The Lord of the Rings* against *The Three Musketeers*, I wish I knew how they'd organized that, enormous interest in the stalls, I can see plenty of denarii changing hands down at the bookmaker's corner, and here come the stars, the Musketeers saluting His Imperial Majesty in their debased Frankish Latin, and now it's the other guys, thank Hera they found a Quenya translator, *nos morituri te salutamus*, always a solemn moment, and they're off! neither side wasting any time here, Frodo has been summoned to an audience with the Queen, here he is, will she be taking him as her new lover, but no! he's showing her the Ring, she's saying something, can't hear what it is, he's given it to her! I must say this is quite unexpected, I suppose she's going to be the new Ringbearer but I can't help feeling that *The Lord of the Rings* is taking a big chance here, by Poseidon! I was right, she's just passed it on to Buckingham, that looks very unwise to me, of course the King wants to know where it is, they're bringing D'Artagnan into play and he's got to cross Rohan to get to England and retrieve the Ring, what's going on here, by Venus's breasts! the impudent pup has insinuated himself into Éowyn's bedchamber and is trying to pass himself off as Aragorn, that will surely never work but no, I can hardly believe it, she's completely fallen for his ruse, I suppose all cats do look the same in the dark! she's found out what's happened and she's trying to stab him with a dagger, D'Artagnan is leaving in a hurry without his breeches and Milady is after him too, things seem grim for him here but wait! Gimli has suddenly chopped off Milady's head with his axe, things are looking up again, D'Artagnan recovers the Ring and heads for Calais and then Mount Doom, climbing the mountain with Porthos and Aramis, I think Athos ducked out and has taken the boat from the Grey Havens, D'Artagnan now almost at the Cracks of Doom, he's going to throw the Ring in but, Zeus and Hera! Sméagol tried the standard diversion and D'Artagnan just pushed him in, he's hijacked a rescue eagle and he's heading for Paris, he's going to give it to Richelieu! what an amazing turnaround, *The Lord of the Rings* seemed to have it in the bag and now it's all over for them, Richelieu receives the Ring and promotes D'Artagnan to First Nazgûl, utter defeat for *The Lord of the Rings*, angry scenes down at the bookmaker's, signing off now.

The History Boys
Alan Bennett

IRWIN: So, what do we think of *The History Boys* then?

RUDGE: It's a classroom drama, sir. Set in Yorkshire during the early 80s. Features a clash between two different styles of teaching, embodied by the two contrasting teachers, Mr. Hector and Mr. Irwin, who ...

IRWIN: Yes, yes, yes, everyone will write that. I am results-focussed, Mr. Hector teaches you the true value of culture. Perfect if you want to get into Bristol. Ideal for Sheffield. Someone else?

SCRIPPS: It's got witty and inventive dialogue, sir.

IRWIN: Such as? You need a striking example, you know.

DAKIN: Mr. Hector calls me "sad" at one point, sir. Mrs. Lintott corrects him, and says she prefers the word "cuntstruck". She points out that it's a compound adjective.

IRWIN: That's better!

DAKIN: It's characteristic of the play to mix highbrow and lowbrow humor, sir. There's a similar joke at the end. I proposition you very directly, and then I note that "my sucking you off" is a gerund. Sir.

IRWIN: Ah, yes, well ...

CROWTHER: Sir, are you blushing? I just thought that might be an interesting detail.

IRWIN: If I am blushing, it is at your naïveté in believing that a few rude words will get you into Oxbridge. You'll have to try harder.

[FIONA enters left, wearing a tight sweater that accentuates her well-developed breasts. She smiles at DAKIN and exits right]

LOCKWOOD: *[sotto voce to AKTHAR]* What was that about?

AKTHAR: *[ditto]* Bleeding obvious, innit?

POSNER: *[taking advantage of momentary confusion]* Sir, can we have a poetic interlude?

OTHER STUDENTS: Oh yes sir, please sir, can we?

IRWIN: Very well. A short one.

POSNER: *[Moves to front, and clasps his hands behind his back]*

> One and another
> In money and guns may outpass his brother;
> And men in their millions float and flow
> And seethe with a million hopes as leaven;
> And they win their will; or they miss their will;
> And their hopes are dead or are pined for still;
> But who'er can know
> As the long days go
> That to live is happy, has found his heaven.
>
> Is it so hard a thing to see
> That the spirit of God — whate'er it be —
> The law that abides and changes not, ages long,
> The Eternal and Nature-born: these things be strong?
> What else is Wisdom? What of Man's endeavor,
> Or God's high grace so lovely and so great?
> To stand from fear set free? To breathe and wait?
> To hold a hand uplifted over Fate?
> And shall not Loveliness be loved for ever?

IRWIN: *[unwilling to admit that he has been moved by the poem]* Where's that from?

POSNER: It's Gilbert Murray's translation of Euripides, sir. Quoted in Shaw's *Major Barbara*. And no sir, it's not actually in the script.

IRWIN: Who's been reading you Euripides?

POSNER: Mr. Hector, sir.

IRWIN: *[Pause, then trying to regain control of the situation]* Well ... we still need to establish what this play is about. Anyone?

CROWTHER: Ah, sir, as Rudge said, it's largely about the clash between you and Mr. Hector. He lacks imagination, and persists in the tired old traditions of the British Empire, believing that a broad knowledge of Culture is sufficient grounding for life.

IRWIN: Good! Good! Go on!

CROWTHER: You sir, on the other hand, grasp the fact that true understanding requires constant questioning of established beliefs. Even though this questioning may at first appear no more than mechanically contrarian, it is a kind of spiritual exercise which ultimately instills a flexible and dynamic way of thinking appropriate to the modern world.

IRWIN: Excellent! Any more observations?

CROWTHER: Well, sir, I think we're pretty much out of time. Now we need an unexpected tragedy to wrap things up.

IRWIN: You're right. *[He suddenly has a massive heart attack, and falls lifeless to the floor. POSNER, tears in his eyes, attempts unsuccessfully to revive him]*

LOCKWOOD: This isn't in the script either, is it?

SCRIPPS: *[Sitting down at piano]* No.

[He begins to play "L'amour est un oiseau rebelle" from Carmen. The OTHER STUDENTS gather around the body of IRWIN. Curtain]

If Le marin de Gibraltar were a woman
Marguerite Duras

— Yo, DUDE!

— Uh, sorry. I didn't see you.

— I've been waving to you for the last five minutes.

— Um ... I was thinking about something else.

— And where've you BEEN? I've called a bunch of times, and you never get back to me.

— Oh, you know, busy ...

— Who is she?

— What?

— You heard me.

— Uh, her name is Le.

— Is she Vietnamese?

— Well, sort of — no, really she's French. Her full name is Le Marin de Gibraltar. She ...

— Dude, you look like shit. Let me get us a couple of beers. And something to eat.

— It's okay ...

— Waitress! Two beers and a nachos supreme. Thank you. Now tell me about her. Is she cute?

— Mm. No, not really. She's sort of the opposite in fact, she makes no effort at all. When I first met her, I wondered if she was a lesbian. But after a while she kind of grows on you. She ...

— Dude, you sure go for the weird ones. So what's she like?

— Well, she's very intense. She's had this difficult life, with all these substance abuse problems and these messed-up relationships and she's always talking about it. Half the time I'm not even sure she knows I'm there.

— She sounds like trouble to me.

— Yeah.

— But she's fun? In a weird way?

— Um ... let me think. Not that either really. A lot of the time she's just ... boring. She's carrying on and on about her memories and her feelings and I have to be careful not to look at my watch.

— So dude, excuse me for asking, but WTF do you see in her?

— It's a bit hard to explain. It's like, I think she's paying no attention to me, she's just in her own world, and then ...

— And then what?

— It's like ... it's like she can suddenly see into my mind. She tells me exactly what I was thinking, only I didn't even know I was thinking it. I'm completely connected to her. And then we have this amazing, dreamlike sex.

— Wow.

— Yeah.

— She still sounds like a shitload of trouble.

— Yeah.

— Say, what happened to that chick you were dating for a while? Pat? Is that right?

Pattern Recognition And Machine Learning.

— What *is* it with you and these names?

— My first girlfriend was called Enchanted Castle. Hippie parents.

— Whatever. Look, why don't you call up Pat again? You said you got on really well.

— I like her! But I sort of feel Le is better for my soul.

— Dude, you know what? You should give your soul a rest for a while. Call Pat.

— Maybe you're right. I'm sorry, I gotta go. Thanks for the beer.

— Okay. Later, dude.

— Later.

Sherlock Holmes meets The Little Prince
Arthur Conan Doyle and Antoine de Saint-Éxupery

It was some time during the summer of 19— that I received an urgent telegram from Holmes. Arriving at 221B, Baker Street, I was struck by how little he had changed. He was older, to be sure; but his eye was as keen as ever, and his enthusiasm not one whit abated by the passage of the years.

"I trust you have brought your passport, Watson?" he said, in lieu of greeting. "We depart for Algeria this evening. The cab will be here momentarily."

"But Holmes!" I protested, as he hurried me down the stairs. "What —"

"We can discuss that once we are on the train," replied Holmes firmly. And, true to his word, he said no more until we were comfortably ensconced in the First Class carriage of the Dover Express.

"Now, Watson," said Holmes, after he had carefully packed and lit his pipe, "I wonder if you have heard of a young Frenchman called Saint-E——. An author and aviator."

The name was, indeed, familiar, and I said so.

"He was a promising fellow," said Holmes. "Was, I fear, is the correct word. His body was discovered in the Sahara yesterday by a member of the Ain Salah Desert Patrol. The man's commanding officer happened to owe me a small favour, and, knowing my penchant for curious cases, contacted me at once. He says he has taken considerable pains to make sure that the scene is exactly as it was when the poor chap was discovered. If we make the 22.45 ferry, I calculate that we will be there by Wednesday morning."

We arrived at the ferry with a minute to spare. I will not weary my readers with further particulars of the journey, which was arduous though uneventful, but rather continue my narrative at the point when, led by a native guide, we reached Saint-E————'s final resting place. The scene was, indeed, as the Algerian patrolman had found it. I knew from my war-time experience in Afghanistan that the desert air frequently has the property of delaying putrefaction, and Saint-E——— seemed almost to be asleep. He was stretched out on the sand, his head resting on a small knapsack. Only the sightless eyes, apparently fixed on the horizon, revealed his condition. By his right hand was a leather-bound book, which had the appearance of a journal.

Holmes bent down and carefully picked it up. Together, we examined the pages: in strange and poetic prose, Saint-E——— told us the sad story of his last days.

"Well, Watson," said Holmes after we had concluded our perusal of the manuscript. "What conclusions can we draw from this unusual tale?"

I am not ashamed to say that I had to brush away a few drops of moisture from my eyes. "My dear Holmes, it is obvious!" I replied. "The poor fellow, evidently dying of thirst, had fallen prey to the hallucinations that are so common in these parts. How else to explain this fantastic tale of a young visitor from another world?"

"I must disagree," said my friend firmly. "Look again at the illustrations. For example, this fine picture of a planetoid consumed by three baobab trees. Could this careful, painstaking draftsmanship be the product of a man in the grip of fevered visions?"

"You are right," I said reluctantly. "But, if his tale is not a dream, then what can it be? Surely you are not suggesting that the unfortunate M. Saint-E——— was actually visited by a person from the stellar regions?"

"You know my methods," replied Holmes. "When one has eliminated the impossible, then whatever remains, no matter how implausible, must be true. We have established that the deceased was not hallucinating when he wrote these words. Evidently, he cannot have met a visitor from another world. Suppose, however, that he met someone who successfully convinced him he was such a person?"

"But," I expostulated, "who could this person be? And what motive would they have had for perpetrating such an outlandish deception on a dying man?"

"I beg to draw your attention," said Holmes, "to the curious condition of the aviator's aircraft. It is odd, do you not agree?"

"But there is no aircraft!" I said, exasperated.

"That," said Holmes, "is precisely the curious condition to which I refer. The non-existence of the aircraft appears to require some explanation."

I clapped my hand to my brow in consternation. It was indeed as Holmes said: up to that moment, I had not noticed the aviator's signal lack of visible transport. My friend continued his exposition.

"You may possibly have had occasion," he said, "to read my monograph on North African secret societies. If you have, you will perhaps recall the one the Tuareg call the Meyy-Dupp, and the French the Figue-Tiscieux. They are notorious for their use of imaginative midget accomplices, generally dressed in fanciful costumes. They appear to travellers in the deep desert, and inveigle their way into their confidence. After spinning a fantastic web of lies, they drug the victim and then summon the main band, who make away with the unfortunate man's possessions, leaving him to die a miserable death in the sands. I fear that poor Saint-E—— has met just such a fate."

"But Holmes," I stammered. "What ... how ... "

"As it happens," Holmes said casually, "I suspected this might be the case. My friends at Ain Salah located a Meyy-Dupp encampment only an hour's march from here. They found the pieces of Saint-E——'s airplane and a midget dressed in exactly the clothes shown in these pictures. The miscreants have been arrested and are presently in safe custody awaiting trial."

"Holmes," I said, "This is simply extraordinary! Please tell me ..." But my friend was no longer listening.

"We must get back to England at once," he snapped. "I have just learned that Moriarty has been sighted again."

The Godfather
Mario Puzo

— Come in.

— Ah, Don Corleone, I'm sorry to trouble you —

— Sit down.

— Thank you, Don Corleone —

— Where is your mother from?

— I'm sorry?

— Your mother, she is from Italia. Which town?

— Ah, she's from Perugia.

— Perugia. Yes. Bacci di Perugina. I like those chocolates. You call yourself Manny. Why?

— I'm named after my great-grandfather, Emmanuele —

— Emmanuele. A good Italian name. I will call you that. Well, Emmanuele, how many books have you reviewed on Goodreads?

— Ah, I'm not quite sure —

— Tom, how many reviews?

— I believe 623, Don Corleone.

— So. Emmanuele. Your mother is from Perugia. You have reviewed 623 books. Why do you come to me first now?

— Well, Don Corleone, I —

— No. I understand. You felt that the, how do you say, the literary quality was not so high. But you are running out of books. You want votes. Now, you come to me, you want to be my friend. Am I right?

— Ah, Don Corleone, of course I would like votes, but —

— It's alright. Clemenza?

— Yes, Don Corleone?

— Make sure that Emmanuele gets some votes for this review.

— Yes, Don Corleone.

— Don Corleone, I don't know how to thank you. I —

— One day I will ask you to repay me. Until then, don't worry. I see there is something else you want to ask.

— Ah, yes Don Corleone, but I'm not sure —

— You may ask me. What is your question?

— Well, Don Corleone. Are you ... are you God?

— Luca, it's okay. He's writing a review. He's allowed to ask me that. Emmanuele, why this question?

— Ah, they call you the Godfather. You're very powerful but very just and kind, as long as people are utterly loyal to you. You have a son, called Sonny. He's killed. But then Michael comes back, and everyone says he's exactly like you. And Mario Puzo seems to be fond of this theme. He wrote the script for *Superman*, and it's a bit similar. Jor-El is also like God, and he sends his son to Earth to save mankind, and somehow although Jor-El is dead, he lives on in Kal-El, Superman.

— I see. These are interesting questions. I will ask Signor Puzo next time I see him.

— But ... Don Corleone, will he tell you?

— He will. I'm going to make him an offer he can't refuse.

Go Ask Alice
Beatrice Sparks

— Alice? They told me to go ask you.

— Ask me what?

— Ah ... I guess, should I do drugs?

— Well, how would I know? I'm just a made-up girl in a piece of anti-drugs propaganda that somehow became more famous than it deserved.

— Hey, don't be like that. I meant, if you actually had existed, then what would you have said?

— I'd have said, aren't you a bit old to be asking me this question? Why didn't you stop by over 30 years ago?

— I did!

— And what did I say?

— You said, don't do drugs, or you'll get addicted and totally fuck your life up and die a miserable death in your early 20s lying on a filthy mattress in some hippy squat ...

— And?

— And what?

— Did you do drugs?

— Um, yes, I did.

— So did you die a miserable death in your early 20s?

— Well, obviously not. I just decided after one slightly unpleasant experience that I didn't like them much, and stopped.

— You didn't feel an irresistible craving to start again, even though you knew it made no sense?

— I'm afraid I didn't.

— Look, I meant well, you know? To the extent that a fictional character can mean anything.

— It's okay, Alice. We're cool. Nice talking to you.

— Bye! Oh yes, I almost forgot, tell your son to read me.

— Um, he doesn't even like alcohol much, and he only really reads military history books. I'd be embarrassed.

— Never mind. Stop by sometime and we'll have a few drinks and talk about classic trash literature.

— Thanks Alice! Sounds like fun. I might take you up on that.

— Bye!

Scott Pilgrim versus The World
Bryan Lee O'Malley

David dragged us to see the movie on Saturday. Elisabeth slumbered fitfully, waking up occasionally to see if it was getting any better and generally deciding it wasn't. I thought it was interesting at an abstract level, and I found several scenes funny or sexy, but I had to admit that I couldn't really appreciate it. I also felt rather sleepy at times. David looked both superior and a little embarrassed. "Well, it's really a movie for my generation," he admitted.

The startling realisation that struck me about ten minutes in is that *video games have now become culture!* Since I've never played Mortal Kombat or anything similar, it was like watching a movie in a foreign language. Admittedly a language where I had some passive vocabulary, but none the less. I had to hand it to them — structuring a romcom as a video game was clever, and judging from other people's reactions it worked. Several times, I caught myself thinking that, if only I'd known, I would have done a bit of Tekken first to get the literary background. You know, like reading *The Odyssey* before attacking *Ulysses*, or *Mrs Dalloway* before *The Hours*.

On the way home, we wondered if this was the start of a paradigm shift. (We'd just read *The Shallows* ...) There's a logical progression, I argued. Don Quixote sees life as a medieval romance. Tom Sawyer sees it as a Dumas novel. Us twentieth century people see it as a movie. (Cue the violins! Let's ride off together into the sunset!) So, really there's nothing odd about imagining it as a video game. Now that I think about it, there have been plenty of advance warnings; *The Matrix* springs to mind, and there was that wonderful moment in *Four Lions* where the suicide bomber wonders if he'll get bonus points for additional victims, like in *XBox Counterstrike*. I guess this is just the most flagrant example yet.

But I do wonder if the trend is going to continue. And to what extent is *Scott Pilgrim* exaggerating? Do people born in the 90s, or at least some of them, *really* see romance as a video game? My heart tells me it's impossible: romance can only be a book, a movie or a piece of music! But I'm prepared to be corrected. New generation readers, please give me your honest thoughts! I'm curious.

[Medium shot. Morning, grubby kitchen. MANNY and OLDER CHICK are sitting at breakfast table drinking coffee]

[Box attached to OLDER CHICK says:

Name: none of your business

Age: none of your business

Fun fact: still kinda hot]

MANNY: So now I've actually read it.

OLDER CHICK: Read what? And why does this box say I'm still kinda hot? Why shouldn't I be?

MANNY: You're, like, older. You're over 25.

[Close-up of OLDER CHICK rolling oversized manga eyes]

OLDER CHICK: Give me a break. And you can't do Scott Pilgrim dialogue. There's more to it than just adding "like" every now and then.

[Close-up of MANNY shrugging]

MANNY: Well I wanted to show I was starting to appreciate it. I'm acquiring some familiarity with the conventions. Like.

[Even closer, huge eyes, in need of haircut]

MANNY: I realize I'm finding it ... FUNNY!!

[Back to OLDER CHICK, suddenly smiling]

OLDER CHICK: Well you go for it. At least you described me

as kinda hot. Come here.

[Medium shot. MANNY and OLDER CHICK embrace]

KISSY KISSY KISSY

[OLDER CHICK pulls back, looks thoughtful]

OLDER CHICK: Say, who am I anyway? Your wife?

MANNY: I thought I'd leave that deliberately ambiguous. To heighten the dramatic tension.

OLDER CHICK: You're not fooling anyone.

[Close-up. MANNY and OLDER CHICK embrace again]

KISSY KISSY KISSY

[MANNY pulls back. Close-up]

MANNY: I'm amazed. I'm suddenly into this genre. It's like learning to read Proust.

[Close-up, from underneath]

MANNY: Except it takes an afternoon instead of several months.

[Close-up of OLDER CHICK]

OLDER CHICK: Does that mean it's, like, shallow? And who's she?

[Camera backs off. An EVIL EX-GIRLFRIEND has entered the room]

MANNY: Looks like an evil ex-girlfriend.

OLDER CHICK: I suppose I have to fight her?

MANNY: If you feel up to it.

[Several panels of OLDER CHICK and EVIL EX-GIRLFRIEND engaging in exaggerated video game violence]

[Close-up of OLDER CHICK]

OLDER CHICK: Sorry, this isn't my metaphor of choice.

[Close-up of EVIL EX-GIRLFRIEND]

EVIL EX-GIRLFRIEND: Not mine either.

[Close-up of MANNY]

MANNY: You're right. Let's do Proust intead.

[Medium shot. OLDER CHICK, EVIL EX-GIRLFRIEND and MANNY are now dressed like 1890s French aristocrats. The grubby kitchen has become a tasteful reception room]

OLDER CHICK: I presume we will see you at the Duchesse's ball on Saturday?

[Label pointing to OLDER CHICK's speech bubble: "Totally under-the-belt ninja-style attack move!"]

MANNY: Plus ça change, n'est pas?

253: A Novel

Geoff Ryman

On 02:53 on the 25th of March, it so happened that there were exactly 253 people in the world reading Geoff Ryman's novel. For 253 seconds, each of them *[Get on with it — Ed]*. Oh yes. Here are some of their stories.

4. KEITH PERZ

Keith, a graceless, limp-haired student, lives in Seattle, WA. He is writing a dissertation on *253*. His girlfriend, Miranda, had suggested the idea to him a few weeks ago, and he gratefully accepted.

Now Miranda has just left him, and he's stuck. The dissertation is due tomorrow. Keith is in the middle of a paragraph that starts like this:

> A normal novel is structured along the temporal dimension; the author takes a small number of people, and follows their evolution through an extended period of time. Ryman, in contrast, asks why a novel cannot be structured along the dimension of space; he takes a small number of minutes, and traces the evolution of an extended set of people through that interval. The point, one realises at the end,

Keith is unable to finish the sentence: no words come to him. He wonders whether Miranda intentionally sold him an impossible topic, and is suddenly convinced she has done so. He begins to weep.

13. DOROTHEA KRIEGH

Dorothea, an elderly lady who works a part-time cleaning job in Boston, has not read a book in four years. She had forgotten that she could enjoy reading, but she found *253* abandoned on a park bench earlier that evening as she walked home. Now she can't stop turning the pages. So many people, so many tangled lives! She has a remarkably good memory despite her advanced age, and avidly connects the threads together. So that was what the Indian lady's husband was doing!

She wants to capture some of the thoughts that are whirling around in her tired brain. She takes a pencil and writes:

People are all so different but they are all the same.

But this doesn't really express what she intended. She looks at her words, momentarily dissatisfied, then goes back to reading.

22. TOM FORSTER

Tom, a bright and oversexed British 11 year old, has stolen the book from his older brother. Andy's books sometimes contain racy material. Their parents have installed a family filter on their internet connection and strictly monitor their reading matter, but Andy has discovered strategies for outwitting security.

Tom has just flipped his way to a page where another teenage boy is fantasizing about having oral sex with an older woman. He reads the passage four times, trying to extract every drop of excitement from it. Then he opens Microsoft Word on his laptop and types the single word:

CUNT

He has an erection.

35. MIRANDA WANG

Miranda, a beautiful, petite Chinese-Canadian girl, lives in Vancouver, BC. She has just broken up with her boyfriend Keith, whom she has been dating for a little more than a year. She can't quite decide why she told him she was leaving; she was just tired of him. She feels bad. She shouldn't have done it the day before his dissertation was due.

She opens her iPhone and writes a mail to her friend Amy:

> okay i took your advice. gave him a great idea for his paper anyway. 253 is the best you read it girl.

She is suddenly more comfortable with her decision. She's hurt him, but she inspired him at the same time. She feels she has class.

47. MANNY RAYNER

Manny, a middle-aged academic currently resident in Switzerland, is addicted to the Goodreads website. He should have gone to bed hours ago, but is suffering from toothache, an unfamiliar condition. He had hoped that reading *253* would help him doze off. To his disappointment, he's more awake than ever. He decides to write a review:

> On 02:53 on the 25th of March, it so happened that there were exactly 253 people in the world ...

Overqualified
Joey Comeau

Geneva
Switzerland
February 17, 2012

Dear Goodreads,

I am applying for the position of Advertising Sales Director and I enclose a copy of my resume. I have no previous experience in advertising or sales, but I hope you will view my qualifications from a broader perspective.

Goodreads, I understand Internet addiction. I know what it's like to get up at three in the morning because you can't sleep and your life is falling apart and how you log on to a useless shitty social networking site because you're too stressed out and brain-dead to be able to think of something more positive to do. I know how you click refresh thirty-four times before you see a new item in your update feed, and then I know how you spend the next two hours chatting with some moron who hasn't read anything but Harry Potter in his entire life and can't even spell, because you've fucked up all your other relationships and you have no one else to talk to. And then when you've insulted this poor Potter fan so much that he won't talk to you either, I know how you spend another hour looking for a LOLcat you can post that will enable you to say you've won the argument.

Goodreads, I know from the inside what motivates these people. I would be able to channel their emptiness and depair into commercially profitable activities, like buying crap books they will never open or paying to access porn sites that will show you some woman with a bad boob job and an eating disorder and bags under her eyes that her pancake makeup is unable to hide, listlessly playing with her pussy and pretending she's still got some vestigial sex appeal. I would be able to convince your clients that you are an organization worth investing in. They would listen respectfully and take out their checkbooks and we would all become richer.

Hire me.

Manny Rayner

Vox
Nicholson Baker

There's such a diversity of opinions concerning this book that I can't bring myself to take sides. Instead, I present:

Your cut-out-and-keep do-it-yourself Vox reviewing kit
This (ground-breaking/tedious/overhyped/short) novel does for phone sex what (*Last Tango in Paris/Lady Chatterley's Lover/ Death in the Afternoon/ The Bell Jar/Ben Hur*) did for (sodomy/ gamekeepers/bullfighting/suicide/chariot-racing). Nicholson Baker's book is (surprisingly/predictably/tediously/unnecessarily) (sensitive/pornographic/dull/engaging), and (shows how true intimacy is independent of medium/offers insightful commentary on sex in a post-AIDS society/presents a tired collection of masturbatory clichés/goes through the motions of pretending to entertain) as it builds towards a climax which (is both sexually arousing and emotionally moving/shows the protagonists coming noisily all over the page/should have happened 50 pages earlier/was as drearily predictable as the rest of the book).

(Warmly/Reluctantly/Not) recommended to (anyone who's ever been in love/dirty-minded pseudo-intellectual poseurs/teenagers with strict but short-sighted parents).

Part VI
Chess and Other Geekiness

Are You A Geek?
Tim Collins

A few questions that didn't make it into this book:

What is the funniest thing you've ever read?

— *Three Men in a Boat*. (0 points)

— Terry Pratchett's *Discworld* series. (1 point)

— Terry Pratchett's *Discworld* series, and you then list all 38 books in order of how funny you think they are. (3 points)

— Roger Penrose's *The Road to Reality*. The way he disses the string theorists is hysterical, needless to say, but the high point is the section where he gets confused about K-meson decay. That just had me ROFLing. (5 points)

Someone at a party is telling the man-with-a-wooden-leg-named-Smith joke from *Mary Poppins*. What do you do?

— Laugh and say you'd forgotten that bit. (0 points)

— Repeat "A man with a wooden leg named Smith!" several times in the Older Mr. Dawes's voice, and remind people that he was also played by Dick Van Dyke. (1 point)

— Say that the humor of the joke depends on an attachment ambiguity, and explain how, when you were still at high school, you wrote a program that could find both grammatical parses. (5 points)

Do you play first-person shoot-em-ups on your laptop?

— No, they're a waste of time. (0 points)

— Yes, but I try to limit myself to less than four hours a day. (1 point)

— No, I think internet speed chess is more exciting and violent than any video game yet invented. (3 points)

— Yes, internet speed chess is no good since everyone cheats by using chess engines. (5 points)

— No, I've gone back to playing internet speed chess since ICC brought in software to check for people using chess engines. (7 points)

— Yes, I stopped playing chess on ICC after I found that I could write a program which combined the outputs of three different chess engines to fool the security filters. (10 points)

Why didn't you write this book instead of Tim Collins?

— I'm not geeky enough. (0 points)

— I'm not funny enough. (1 point)

— I'm geeky and funny enough, but I spend all my time searching for errors in Penrose and writing software to fool the security filters on ICC. (3 points)

— I'm so geeky that even the average geek thinks I'm too geeky to be amusing. (5 points)

— I did write this book, but Tim Collins ripped it off and published it under his name, removing all the best questions. (10 points)

Revolution in the 70s meets Fahrenheit 451

Garry Kasparov and Ray Bradbury

Garry Kasparov's books are always seething with emotion, but it's a little hard to see that if you're not a chessplayer yourself. This book is a drenched-in-nostalgia look at the 70s, the Golden Age of chess analysis. Fischer had just captured the world title mainly due to his stunning opening preparation. Under his influence, top players everywhere — but particularly in the Soviet Union — were busily creating new systems. Kasparov tells you about their exciting discoveries — the Hedgehog, the Sveshnikov Variation, the resurgent Petrov Defence, Larsen's reinterpretation of the Meran, and many more.

And now all these lands are under the wave ... with grandmaster-level software generally available, anyone can be a chess analyst. The rigorous clarity that Kasparov so painfully acquired is obsolete. It's very tragic. So, in an attempt to provide subtitles, here's:

If *Revolution in the 70s* **Had Been Written By Ray Bradbury**

"What's your name?" Montag asked.

"Cassie," she said. "I'm your neighbour. We moved in a few weeks ago."

"And what do you do?" he continued, not knowing what else to say.

"I'm a chessplayer," she said defiantly. "Or, more exactly, a chess analyst."

Unconsciously, he took a step backwards, and she laughed.

"Oh, don't worry. I don't have any chess books, if that's what you're thinking. Just a database and some playing engines."

He hadn't noticed that he was holding his breath, and now he exhaled.

"Yes," she said with sudden bitterness, "I analyse using Fritz and Junior and Rybka. Though sometimes I switch them off and move the pieces around myself. If the position appears to warrant it. That's still allowed, you know."

"But ... aren't the machines more accurate?" asked Montag, unable to restrain himself.

"Oh, they are," said the girl softly. "They are. I always use them to check my lines. I'd be very foolish not to."

"So they're a good thing, really?" said Montag, feeling that he might be on firmer ground.

"It depends on what you want," said Cassie, looking directly at him for the first time. "If you're after the truth, you should use the machines. But they don't give you the feeling of discovering something by yourself. That's why I became a chessplayer. I used to be a researcher and an artist. Now I'm just another office worker."

Montag had no idea what to reply to this. She was still looking at him, but he wasn't sure who she was speaking to.

"When I was little," continued the girl, "I used to read my father's copies of *Informator*. He had a complete set. At the beginning of every number, there was a list of the Ten Best Games and the Ten Best Theoretical Novelties of the last one. The Ten Best New Moves. I used to dream that one day I would find one of those new moves, and my name would be there too."

"And did you?" asked Montag.

"They stopped printing *Informator* when I was eleven," said the girl. "But I learned something important from it. All the chess games that have ever been played are just moves in one big game. That's why I loved chess theory. I wanted to be part of that game."

"But you are, aren't you?" said Montag uncertainly. "I mean, if you're a chess analyst."

The girl studied him carefully. "Not really," she said. "My machine is part of the game. But I'm not."

Montag thought he had never heard anyone sound so sad. He looked for some comforting words, but the only things that came to mind were advertising jingles and greeting cards.

"I'm sorry," said the girl, suddenly formal. "I've taken up too much of your time. It was nice talking to you."

She held out her hand. Montag shook it mechanically.

When he got home, his wife was watching the TV wall as usual. "You're a little late, dear," she said. "Was your train delayed again?"

"I was talking with the girl from next door," said Montag. "She's a chessplayer." But then he noticed that Mildred was wearing her seashells, so he didn't say anything else.

The Integral Trees
Larry Niven

Integrating the trees $f(z)$ around the Smoke Ring C, we have

$$\oint_C f(z)dz = \oint_C \frac{1}{(z^2+1)^2}dz$$

$$= \oint_C \frac{\frac{1}{(z+i)^2}}{(z-i)^2}dz = 2\pi i \frac{d}{dz}\left(\frac{1}{(z+1)^2}\right)\bigg|_{z=i}$$

$$= 2\pi i \left(\frac{-2}{(z+1)^3}\right)\bigg|_{z=i} = 2\pi i \frac{1}{4i} = \frac{\pi}{2}$$

But since the plot is strictly monotonous, we easily obtain

$$\text{point} = 0$$

and hence

anything Niven wrote before Ringworld Engineers $\gg$ this dreary mess I couldn't even finish

QED

Next week, we prove from first principles that there are at most 867 books in the Man-Kzin Wars series.

Finnegans Wake
James Joyce

The other day we saw *The Ghost*, the rather fine new movie by Polanski. Ewan McGregor plays a ghostwriter, who's been brought in to fix up the memoirs of a British ex-Prime Minister who absolutely isn't Tony Blair. He's given the manuscript, and groans in pain.

"That bad?" asks the woman who isn't Cherie Blair.

"Well it's got all the words," says McGregor. "They're just not in the right order."

This suggested to me the following simple experiment with *Finnegans Wake*, one of the greatest etc etc in the English language. I downloaded an electronic version from the Web and wrote a little script. It calculates statistics for the frequencies of each letter conditioned on the three preceding ones, then produces random text using that model. And here's a sample of what comes out:

> rivin's Fleperumpholature, puirel from the going beamstroki, genes aultealsion! Captermidcauting. Allfishe'll theiresendt all, andfall the blisation (for of ally witnes of coulminus. Blugger, wher nutbrings my los oned? Mch? What sting up funnies! Huddamsome Bankata, the keter soother sets the beloomostes, sable us in duallects neupon, wholy not does! Exceed in siltop as taned mucheepiworder aflute. While store your bred welchups we kitch oxbell, old som! Curly vale. The scenty view (the our civisierengracles was dupshua milisquewing bransisterrand the knobo, prise fall knacordy) and picky karu? Yip! I sait is, worts fore fassoo thath they speechappy inted that bit thall kning to thehry. For the like fing of the untill Buggedy Acreside? Byg-

mour flatehaun sore! But a cal, them doland up (and you, perfor virging of the Gachind lilt and supping's the that the saint, him my brade rainpleave you abothe king Jerospears forews wer's vitrodalths vitation abou remen thorly wated bease, there lit is like the Lucat wattern-his in thing hone: he willwho it bynemberumphs, faraden, here they sail nought of the sweet-puls temple of are whirk and eld not and Palm aro! This evers, Exmoonanture, thead fied and too tron the lanagain ther! Marre! Kevitutterod. Shaughter of Eons, Potter rud of thin collow. One to beehights headlos he gue. Dalilitopspes hers and a Noho. All to evers scan night!

Juva: Sod the thurch he breated! And the ming's my schlucises lausan the coy Brael mudder Sever, a his nakewdy feat Bashoweriful and it feet to mire blowsome, thems bis!

OK, I admit it's not as accomplished as the original. But if you brought in a competent ghostwriter and gave him a month to improve it, who knows? The random generator has created some promising lines. I quite like "For the like fing of the untill Buggedy Acreside?", and "Juva: Sod the thurch he breated!" seems interestingly blasphemous ...

Kasparov v Karpov 1986-1987 meets Black Swan

Garry Kasparov and Darren Aronofsky

I was trying to think how I could present this marvellous study in paranoia and obsession to the non-chess-playing reader — and, the very same day, we saw *Black Swan*.

Well, after that it was obvious. Just close your eyes and try to imagine Garry Kasparov in a tutu ...

DRAMATIS PERSONAE

GARRY KASPAROV .... Natalie Portman
ANATOLY KARPOV .... Mila Kunis
KLARA KASPAROVA ...... Barbara Hershey
MIKHAIL BOTVINNIK ..... Vincent Casel
BOBBY FISCHER .... Winona Ryder
EDWARD WINTER .... Himself

Scene 1

[BOTVINNIK is drilling KASPAROV and the OTHER BALLERINAS]

BOTVINNIK: One, two, three, four! Plié! Jeté! Queen's Gambit Declined!

[Suddenly, everyone becomes aware of a piece of paper pinned to the noticeboard. The BALLERINAS cluster round]

FIRST BALLERINA: Congratulations, Garry! The Swan Queen — I mean, the World Champion!

SECOND BALLERINA: Every chessplayer's dream role!

[KASPAROV is still stunned, he can't quite believe it]

BOTVINNIK: Garry, we need to talk.

[He takes KASPAROV to one side]

We know you can be the White Swan. You can attack, you can combine, you can dazzle people with your flawless technique. But can you be the Black Swan?

KASPAROV: *[Hesitantly]* I've learned all the steps ...

BOTVINNIK: *[Implacable]* That's not enough. You must be able to maneuver slowly, to allow your opponent to defeat himself, to use dirty tricks ...

KASPAROV: I have to go home. Mom will be worried.

BOTVINNIK: Well, here's some homework for you. The autobiography you're writing, *Child of Change*. I want you to jerk off all over it.

KASPAROV: I was planning to do that anyway.

BOTVINNIK: *[Momentarily disconcerted]* Ah ... good!

[As KASPAROV leaves, KARPOV moves sexily up to BOTVINNIK]

Scene 2

[A few weeks later. KASPAROV has just lost three straight games, one from a winning position. He gazes into the mirror]

KASPAROV: Something's wrong. My Grünfeld Defence is bleeding. *[He picks nervously at it. A large piece of the Smyslov Variation comes off in his hand]* My team is selling opening secrets to Karpov. I have proof.

[He gets into bed and tries to sleep. Suddenly, he notices KLARA KASPAROVA slumped in the chair next to him]

EDWARD WINTER: As a chess historian, I strongly object to this scene! Kasparov's mother only slept in his room during the *first* match, not the third ...

AUDIENCE: Shut up.

KASPAROV: *[Jumps out of bed and smashes mirror]* I need to kill someone. *[Takes shard of glass and stabs invisible person]*

You're fired, Evgenii Vladimirov! *[He collapses unconscious]*

Scene 3

[The match hall just before the start of game 22. KASPAROV, very pale, sits down on one side of the chessboard. KARPOV, sexy and radiant, sits down opposite him]

AUDIENCE: *[Murmuring]* Finished ... cracking up ... Karpov's victory certain ...

[Fantasy sequence. In an incredible series of moves, KASPAROV dances all over the board, slowly ensnaring KARPOV's pieces in an invisible web]

KASPAROV: *[As he dances]* The Black Swan ...

[Dark feathers sprout from KASPAROV's shoulders. He infiltrates a knight to f8 and traps KARPOV's king on h6]

AUDIENCE: *[Murmuring]* Extraordinary ... unbelievable ... like an endgame study ...

[KARPOV, despairing, resigns. The AUDIENCE applaud frantically. KASPAROV leaps off the stage]

KASPAROV: *[Whispers]* Perfect ...

[Fade to white. A pause]

KASPAROV: Am I ... dead?

BOTVINNIK: No, you're playing Karpov again next year in Seville.

KASPAROV: Shit!

Dude, Where's My Country?
Michael Moore

One of the early triumphs of Unified Media Theory was the discovery of the anti-coulter. Predicted in 2001 and experimentally verified the following year, the anti-coulter (often colloquially referred to as the "mooreon") is a heavy particle with positive charm, charge and strangeness and leftward spin. It is unstable, decaying with a half-life of slightly under four years into derivative books and movies. The decay reaction also produces a large number of dollars.

Media physicists at the CNN supercollider hope soon to begin a controversial series of experiments in which coulters and anti-coulters will be accelerated to 99% of the speed of light and smashed into each other. Speculation that this could give rise to a massive black hole and cause the end of the Universe has been dismissed by CNN experts as "unfounded nonsense".

Karpov's Caro Kann: Panov's Attack
Anatoly Karpov and Mikhail Podgaets

If Chess Were Love: An Analogy

Instead of telling you just what it is that Karpov and Podgaets are saying about the Panov attack, which I fear is of limited interest, let me try to explain it in emotional terms. I used to play chess competitively at international level, and opening theory was very important. I'd spend a lot of time reading up on what the top players were doing, researching new moves, discussing them with my friends, and so on. The Panov Attack was an opening I played regularly. Now, I can buy this book, and get hard answers to many questions which I cared deeply about in the 70s. It's fascinating. The only problem is, there's just too much information.

Analogy time! Let's pretend that I had a similar experience in everyday life. I'm asleep one night and I'm granted a direct audience with one of God's angels. Here's me talking to Gabriel:

— Okay Manny, now I know you've wondered many times what would have happened if you'd kissed Sara at that party?

— Uh, yeah.

— Well, she was hoping you would. She was really disappointed you didn't.

— Oh!

— She'd have gone home with you, and you'd have had wild and crazy sex.

— Damn!!

— But two months later, she'd have met your friend Martin and decided she liked him better. She'd have left you and your heart would have been broken.

— Uh, well, then maybe ...

— A week after that, you'd have been in a bookstore, wondering whether to buy *The Alexandria Quartet* or *Fear of Flying*. Which one do you think you'd have chosen?

— Um, I don't know ...

— If you'd bought *Fear of Flying*, you'd immediately have met a Spanish student called Dolores, whose favorite book it was. You'd have left the bookstore with her, and Sara would have seen you together. She'd have felt that she'd made a terrible mistake, and begged you to take her back. Would you have done so?

— Well, ah, maybe ...

— See, if you were too proud to take her back, as you might easily have been, then you'd have married Dolores and moved to Spain. But she'd have died of cancer when she was only 36.

— Um ... what would have happened if I'd bought the other book?

— That's complicated. Where do you think you'd have put it when you got home?

— Ah, I don't know, on the table perhaps?

— In that case, three days later, you'd have randomly opened it at 2.17 am when you were a bit drunk, and you'd have had a surprising thought. It would have made you write a short story that you thought was very good. What would you have done next?

— This is making my head hurt. I have no idea.

— Well, if you'd submitted it to a ...

— I can't handle any more of this. I'm going to wake up now.

— Don't you even want to know what would have happened if you'd taken Sara back in subvariation A2i?

— No. Thanks, but I'll live without it. It was all a long time ago, you know?

— Wait ...

— Gabriel, it was nice meeting you. You're really cool, but I gotta go.

Some people think computer analysis is killing chess. You can kind of see their point.

The Flanders Panel
Arturo Pérez-Reverte

Notgettingenough (also a chessplayer) told me I had to read this, and she was indeed right. I couldn't put it down, and finished it in about a day. It's ... well, what is it? I read it as a kind of postmodernist reimagining of *Alice Through The Looking-Glass*. Other books I immediately thought of were *The Name of the Rose*, *Gödel, Escher, Bach* and *Luzhin's Defense*.

Formally, it's a very stylized murder mystery. Julia, the sexy but childlike Alice figure, is a Madrid art restorer. She receives an unusual commission, a 15th century painting of a chess game. There are multiple layers of reference: two of the people in the painting are playing chess, while the third one, a mysterious lady in black, watches. But they are also identified with the pieces, since it turns out that the picture contains a hidden message about the relationships between them, coded in the position of the game itself. Which in turn is reflected in the mirror shown on one side of the painting.

So, self-reference, reflections, semantics, maps and territories. And, just as in *Looking-Glass*, the chess game escapes into the real world, or possibly the people fall into the chess world, and everything is simultaneously several other things. César, the older man who has known Julia/Alice since she was a little girl and is her dearest friend, stands in for Lewis Carroll, but he is also the murderer. I was reminded of Michael Dibdin's *The Last Sherlock Holmes Story*, where Holmes turns out to be also Moriarty and Jack the Ripper. Muñoz, the strange, emotionless chessplayer who helps Julia, is Sherlock Holmes, William de Baskerville and Luzhin. And I wonder if his name is a coincidence. In 1960, Bobby Fischer had a very surprising loss to an unknown Ecuadorian player called César Muñoz. Their encounter is moderately famous.

One of the best and most unexpected meta-jokes is about the chess itself. I'm a strong chessplayer, so at first I found the game annoying. The author is clearly not very good at chess, and there are some weird moments. Yet, as the play escapes into the real world, and captured pieces become dead bodies, the chess began to make more sense. At the end, the combinations, previously dream-like and impossible, do in fact become more or less coherent, but still only in a very odd way. Who on earth had been advising him? I couldn't understand it, until he finally revealed that he had been getting help from a chess program. As he points out, once we had the Mechanical Turk, where the machine hid a human player; but here, in the looking-glass world, the machine is hidden in the human. So, this is also one of the first novels I've come across that's been composed partly by a computer; and, now I think of it, the association between Julia and the automaton-like Muñoz is yet another reflection. You were given a clue here too.

What a clever, original, beautiful book. Thank you Not!

I woke up this morning and ... of course! It was staring me in the face all along! Watson, how could I have been so blind!

I said that he admitted to receiving help from a machine, and I still think he did. The play at the end has a machine-like quality, and César's admission about his chess computer seems to refer to the author too. But the position in the van Huys painting is a retrograde analysis problem — a chess puzzle where the task is to work out the preceding moves — and no machine can compose a retrograde analysis problem. He needed assistance from a strong human player as well. So the real mystery is not the identity of the murderer, but the question of who composed the problem.

Well ... he certainly gives you plenty of hints. The references to Bach pieces where the composer's name is hidden in the notes. I was sure there was a message hidden here, but I couldn't see it. And consider Julia's two helpers. César is always referred to by his first name, Muñoz always by his last. All of this together is too much to be just an accident.

César Muñoz, step forward and take a bow. You've had a very unusual chess career. You beat Bobby Fischer as black, and you helped write this marvelous book. And you were so modest about your contribution that you were willing for it to remain hidden in this cypher. I wonder if I am the first person to crack the code. I just looked around on Google, and if anyone else has spotted it they've been very quiet. The riddle has been lying there for 21 years, waiting for me, the reader.

Of course, of course! He shows you all those semantic reference diagrams, and insinuates that the game can reach out into the real world. It has! Now *I* am in the picture too!

Applause!!!

Part VII

Science

The Selfish Gene
Richard Dawkins

— What some people seem to find hard to understand is that there's a part of you, in fact the most important part, that's immaterial and immortal. Your body is really no more than a temporary shell for the immortal part, and houses it for a little while until it dies. But what you do during that short time is very important. If you live well, the immortal part of you will become absorbed in something much bigger than you are. It will grow and change and achieve things that you can't even dream of. Start thinking of life in these terms, and you will have a completely new perspective on it.

— Hey, I didn't know you believed in —

— In genes? Well of course I do. What did you think I was talking about?

Bonk
Mary Roach

— George?

— Mmm?

— Don't go to sleep.

— Mmm.

— You *are* going to sleep!

— Mm-mm.

— George, tell me something you did today.

— Um ... I read a book.

— That's better! Move around a bit. Yes, that's right, put your hand there. Good. What book?

— *Bonk*. By Mary Roach.

— That silly book about sex?

— It's not silly! She's really got a lot of interesting things to say!

— Like?

— Ah ... I liked the bit about women's orgasms.

— Guess you don't know much about that. OW!

— Sorry, you asked for it. Now do you want me to tell you what she said about women's orgasms?

— OK. I'm sorry I teased you. Put your hand back there. What did she say?

— Well, she spends a lot of time discussing whether women really do have vaginal orgasms. I didn't understand how many different opinions there were. It's complicated!

— Complicated?

— Alright, so most women have clitoral orgasms. Stroking or

kissing their clit gets them off.

— Certainly works for me. Talking of which ...

— No, wait, let me finish. The question is whether so-called vaginal orgasms are really just clitoral orgasms in disguise. The guy's penetrating her, and it gives her an orgasm, but what's really happening is that he's just indirectly stimulating her clit. So it's not really a vaginal orgasm at all.

— Well, I agree with her. I think that's what's happening. But how could you know for sure?

— Look, that's what's so interesting. There was this French princess. Marie Bonaparte. Her clit was a long way from her vagina, and she never got any vaginal orgasms.

— Did her guy have to go down on her then?

— Um ... I think this was before oral sex was invented. She talked to a bunch of women, and measured how far their clits were from their vaginas, and asked them how sex was for them. She has some French word that means you're a woman whose clit is a long way from her vagina. And ...

— There's a French word that means that??

— There is! Look it up. I told you there was good stuff in this book! Teleclit ... something. *Téléclitoridienne*. Aren't you impressed that I remembered that?

— You're not pronouncing it right.

— Well, how am I supposed to say it?

Téléclitoridienne.

— That's what I said. I think. Anyway, the princess found that most *téléclitoridienne* women didn't enjoy penetrative sex. She wrote a scientific paper about it.

— You're asking me to believe that a princess went around, like a hundred years ago, asking a bunch of women questions about their sex lives and measuring how far their clits were from their pussies, and then published the results in a medical journal?

— I agree, it does sound a bit weird. But that's the way Mary Roach tells the story. The princess was so convinced by her findings that she paid a surgeon to operate on her and move her clit further in, so she could have better sex.

— And did it work?

— Well, no. She never had an orgasm again. He screwed up. But he figured out what he did wrong, and next time it worked.

— What a sad story! George?

— Mmm?

— Do you think I'm *téléclitoridienne*?

— Ah ... well ...

— Could you look?

— OK. Turn that light on. Hm. I think you're *mesoclitoridienne*. Between one and three centimeters. I'm guessing one and a half.

— Oh, what a relief. But I think you should check more carefully.

— Like this?

— Well, I was thinking more like this.

— Can you really measure distances that way?

— George, don't be silly. Of course you can.

— Mmm.

— George?

— Mmm?

— I'm glad I'm not a French princess.

Gravitation
Charles Misner, Kip Thorne and Archibald Wheeler

Look. I don't want to whine or anything, but how come the evolutionary biologists get all the attention when the religious right express opinions on science? Why isn't there a massive campaign to make sure that books like this one get sold with a prominent sticker on the front saying "Gravitation's Just A Theory"? It is, you know. Most schoolchildren don't as much as get told that Intelligent Falling exists, let alone giving it equal air time. And, unless I'm greatly mistaken, there's hardly anyone even trying to address the problem.

It just seems so unfair. Evolution's been pretty solid for over a century now; scientists argue over the details, but that's all. Now look at gravitation. First, Einstein comes along in 1915 and completely turns Newton's theory upside down. (See! It's not called a theory for nothing!) There's no absolute space and time, as Newton thought; instead, matter and energy *create* the frame of reference around them. Black holes are just the extreme case.

But Einstein's theory also turns out to be quite shaky. He didn't think that the Universe was expanding, so he added a fudge factor, the so-called Cosmological Constant. Then, in the 30s, new measurements showed the Universe actually *was* expanding. Oops! Einstein takes out the Constant, calling it the greatest mistake of his career. However, the story's not over yet. In the 90s, still newer measurements reveal that the Universe is expanding too quickly. The Constant is put back in again, though now it's generally referred to as Dark Energy. A good bit of marketing there from the Gravitational Theorists.

Somewhere in the middle, young female astronomer Vera Rubin discovers that stars near the edges of galaxies have an orbital velocity that's way too high, if Gravitational *Theory* is correct. First, her male colleagues tell her she must have screwed up on her observations. (Lady scientists in the audience: does this story sound in any way familiar?) Feisty Vera stuck to her guns, until the experts were forced to admit they were wrong. Then most people decided that there had to be extra, invisible "Dark Matter" present, so that they could keep their Theory. It's still completely unclear what the Dark Matter is. I looked around the other day on Google Scholar and found a paper which tried to estimate the mass of the hypothetical "Dark Matter Particles". Using various clever arguments, the author showed that they should be more massive than electrons, but less massive than small stars. That's a spread of several dozen orders of magnitude, which I personally would have summarized as "we don't know". The paper was accepted for publication in a scholarly journal.

And I'm not even going to start on the complete mess that's resulted from numerous failed attempts to reconcile General Relativity with quantum physics. People have been trying for nearly 80 years, and we still don't have anything plausible. Superstring Theory looked good for a while, but, if there were such a thing as Superstring stock, it would have crashed by now to a fraction of its peak valuation. Come on, Intelligent Design people! Why not focus your attention on a more promising target? And, on the principle of Knowing Your Enemy, start with this book. I'm looking forward to watching the fight, and may the best Theory win!

QED
Richard Feynman

Sometimes, it's too late, but that makes you do it better. You probably imagine that this book is a physics text. Well, it is, but that's not what it *really* is. Really, it's a love letter to a dead woman. Feynman says in his introduction that his friend Alix Mautner had always wanted him to explain quantum electrodynamics to her so that she could understand it, and he'd never gotten around to doing that. Now it was too late. But, somehow, you can see that that only made him want to do it, not just well (he did everything well), but perfectly. If the book was perfect, that would make up for its appearing after Alix was no longer around to read it. It may seem like an odd formula, but it worked for Dante, and it also worked for Feynman.

So, to get maximal enjoyment from QED, you should pretend that you're a mysterious dead woman, sitting in Heaven and reading this missive from your dear friend. You're smiling and shaking your head. It's so Dick! You're dead, and you've been told the secrets of the Universe, so of course you no longer need it — but the little flourishes are all his. So clever and thoughtful of him to take out the complex numbers! After all, arrows are exactly the same as complex numbers, and you can add and multiply them in an obvious way ... or at least, he makes you feel it's obvious. How else would you do it?

He's found such a nice entry point, thinking about the way glass reflects monochromatic light. The fact that a tiny difference in thickness makes a huge difference to the proportion of light reflected simply demands an explanation, and the arrows are the only way to make sense of the data. And then, when you start considering how mirrors and lenses work, the Feynman path-integral happens by itself. Of course! It's the only possible solution. When you were alive, you would have loved this.

The rest of it all fits together too. You'd always wondered what those diagrams meant that he kept drawing! They're quite trivial, once you've absorbed a few straightforward details, like positrons being electrons travelling backwards in time. You would have seen what he was referring to when he said that theory agreed with practice to ten decimal places. And even why it's so much harder to do calculations with subatomic particles than with electrons. The coupling coefficient is much bigger! Naturally. How come you never thought of that while you were still mortal?

At the end, he's even included a few questions about things he hasn't figured out yet. You can't wait for him to arrive, so you can give him the answers. It'll be so funny to see his face when you tell him why a muon is like an electron, only with more mass. He'll wonder how he could ever have missed it.

PS I would just like to make it clear that I'm no way implying that anything improper happened between Richard Feynman and Alix Mautner. As far as I'm aware, their relationship was as chaste as the one between Dante and Beatrice. Muses often seem to work most effectively like that.

Part VIII
Linguistics, Philosophy and Sociology

Wittgenstein of the Camel Squadron
Ludwig Wittgenstein and Captain W.E. Johns

1. Let us consider an individual, we may call him L, who joins a World War I fighter squadron. L says to himself that there is no problem. Aerial combat is merely geometry; one projects the trajectories of the two aeroplanes and the machine-gun bullets, and computes the appropriate times and angles. But when he describes these reflections to his new comrades, he is met with howls of derision. Why?

2. L has committed the error, typical of the *Tractatus*, of too closely identifying the map and the territory. "We make pictures to ourselves of the world," he thinks, oblivious to the fact that these pictures may be hard to paint, especially under combat conditions. His colleagues, however, are well aware of this.

3. "What does it mean to say, 'It is two o'clock on the Sun'?" L may muse aloud, during what he believes is a routine reconnaissance mission. Suppose now that his gunner hears this as "Bandit at two o'clock, out of the Sun". He may congratulate L on his alertness and keen eyesight, particularly if an enemy aircraft does indeed appear from that direction. Under these circumstances, L is well advised to keep quiet, and not elaborate on the background to his remark.

4. We want to say that L has been lucky; he did not "really" communicate the position of the enemy aircraft to his colleague. But, now, suppose instead that a bird had flown past, and attracted the gunner's attention, causing him to look in the "two o'clock" direction. He may say afterwards, "A little birdie told me that the Hun was coming out of the Sun". If his fellow-officers subsequently pay more attention to birds, and are more alert as a result, how would we now describe this?

5. Suppose that a person who enjoyed Biggles books as an

eight year old rereads one after an interval of forty-three years, and believes he sees allusions to theories of meaning and references current in 1917. Our first impulse is to say that this is nonsense; the books are meant to be read by small boys, who are not generally conversant with the principles of semantics.

6. On the other hand, one may then retort that small boys are actively engaging in the process of acquiring language and are all practicing semanticians, whether they know it or not. They are thus unusually receptive to semantics-related humor, even if they may be incapable of describing it in those terms.

7. Of that we cannot speak, thereof we must be silent. But what if the young reader of Biggles were later to acquire a philosophical vocabulary? What would he then say?

Our Magnificent Bastard Tongue
John H. McWhorter

A fantastic book! I have not come across anyone, not even Steven Pinker, who does such a good job of showing you how *exciting* linguistics can be. His bold and unconventional history of the English language was full of ideas I'd never seen before, but which made excellent sense. And, before I get into the review proper, a contrite apology to Jordan. She gave it to me six months ago as a birthday present, and somehow I didn't open it until last week. Well, Jordan, thank you, and I'll try to be more alert next time!

So, the book. I'm a linguist of sorts myself, though a rather different kind to McWhorter: his work has centered around the things that happen to grammar when different languages come into contact with each other, while I use grammar as a way to construct speech-enabled software. But, as you'll see a bit later, the fact that we both give a central place to grammar means that our research directions have more to do with each other than you might first think. In *Our Magnificent Bastard Tongue*, McWhorter looks at the history of the English language from his unusual viewpoint. The language has clearly changed a lot since it came into existence; why did it evolve the way it did? McWhorter's answer is that the big changes happened when speakers of different languages started mingling together. He focuses on three changes of this kind.

Although he doesn't present it in this order, I'm going to go backwards in time; the nearer we are to the present, the more likely we are to have clear facts to work with. So, let's first look at what happened when Old English (Beowolf) turned into Middle English (Chaucer). Although Chaucerian English is rather odd, once you've picked up some vocabulary it isn't that hard to read. It's similar, structurally, to the language we speak today. Beowulf is another matter; you have to learn

Old English as a foreign language, and in particular have some of its grammar explained to you. Big things happened in between Old English and Middle English. When you compare with other Germanic languages, you can describe these changes in detail. Old English had a bunch of grammar that most of these other languages still possess. In particular, like German, it had gender (masculine, feminine, neuter) and case (nominative, accusative, genitive, dative). All that stuff somehow disappeared.

I speak Swedish fluently, and I've wondered many times what happened to gender in English; like nearly all other Indo-European languages, Swedish nouns still have gender. Most historical linguists are unable to explain this, and come up with variants on what McWhorter elegantly describes as "Shitte Happens". (One of the things that make this book so readable is that he's only academic when he feels he needs to be). McWhorter puts it down to the Viking invasions of the 8th and 9th centuries. The Vikings spoke Old Norse, a language related to but quite distinct from Old English. Many words were different, but you can always get used to that; the worst part was those bloody endings, which just didn't match up. McWhorter, who has examined several other examples of this kind of collision (he discusses them in his book *Language Interrupted*), says that there's a common pattern: because people can't deal with the divergences in grammar, the language becomes simplified. In another nice turn of phrase, he says that English "was beaten up by Old Norse", and lost gender and case as a result. A striking piece of evidence comes from Northumbrian dialect. Most of the case endings were different, and disappeared quickly; however, the dative plural happened to be the same in Northumbrian Old English and Old Norse, and that held on much longer.

Moving back again in time, McWhorter considers two more perplexing phenomena in English grammar: our use of "do", and the present tense with "be" and "-ing". Neither of these occur in any other Germanic language. English says "Did you buy a paper?" and "I didn't buy a paper", while Swedish says *Köpte du en tidning?* ("Boughtst thou a paper?") and *Jag köpte inte någon tidning* ("I bought not any paper"). This is the normal Germanic word-order, which you still see frequently in Shakespeare and the King James Bible, alongside the construction with "do". Now, "do" has pushed out the normal Germanic construction altogether. Then there's the normal present tense. In English, you ask "What are you doing?" and I answer "I'm writing". In Swedish, you say *Vad gör du?* ("What dost thou?") and I answer *Jag skriver* ("I write"). Again, completely typical for a Germanic language, and I've often wondered why English is so weird. As does my Swedish wife, who sometimes forgets her English grammar when she's sleepy, and is annoyed to find herself slipping back into a normal Germanic word-order. I've never seen anything approaching a sensible explanation of these facts.

But ... as Holmes says, it was under my nose all along! I lived in South Wales from age 2 to 11, in an area where many people spoke Welsh. We had to sing in Welsh at primary school, and when I went to secondary school I did a year of Welsh. I suppose I could blame my Welsh teacher, but really it was my fault: for some reason, I had decided that Welsh was boring and uncool, and I didn't pay any attention in class. If only I had, I might well have noticed what McWhorter points out here. Welsh, typically for a Celtic language but completely atypically for a Germanic one, uses a word-order which is startlingly similar to the bizarre "do" and "be" + "-ing" which we've had at least since Middle English. I downloaded an introductory Welsh course, and it all came flooding back. Look at these examples:

Dw i'n byw yn Llandudno?
(literally: "Am I-in living in Llandudno?")

Do I live in Llandudno?

Dw i ddim yn byw yn Llandudno.
(literally: "Am I not in living in Llandudno.")
I don't live in Llandudno.

As you can see, *dw* (which, uncannily, is even pronounced rather like English "do"), is performing a grammatical function similar to our "do" and "be". It goes near the beginning of the sentence, and combines with the the verb-noun *byw*, "live", to form a present tense. McWhorter presents his case: Welsh does it this way, no Germanic language except for English does, and you had Welsh and English living side by side for centuries. English was the rulers' tongue, so the subjugated Welsh had to learn to speak it. But they did it in their own way, importing some constructions that were central for them, and they were a majority. Their usages became absorbed into English, and they stuck. It's an appealing story. McWhorter discusses the reasons why the mainstream linguistics community is reluctant to accept his account, and indeed it's not as clearcut as you'd like: the problem is that there is, for many centuries, no written evidence of these constructions occuring in English. McWhorter argues that the written and spoken languages were for a long time widely divergent, comparing with modern cases like Arabic. So it's hard to be certain. But if the alternative is "Shitte happened", I must say that I vastly prefer his explanation.

Going still further back in time, McWhorter considers where the whole Germanic family comes from, and proposes a still more audacious hypothesis; the many words in Germanic that don't occur in other Indo-European languages, and its already simplified grammar, are the result of an infusion from a Semitic language, most likely Phoenician. I would love this to be true, but unfortunately there are no written records at all, and it's very hard to prove anything. It's a fine example, though, of the novel kind of linguistic argument you can develop once you start thinking about languages more dynamically, as things that interact and change each other.

As I said at the beginning, McWhorter's work turns out to be surprisingly relevant to research I'm doing myself. One of the reasons I started looking at him was that I've just finished building the first version of a combined grammar for English and Swedish; that is to say, it's a single grammar which covers both languages. It turns out that English grammar, in a sense we can now make precise, is almost completely contained inside Swedish grammar. "Do" and "be" + "-ing" are two of the very few things that, so to speak, stick out. In the other direction, the things I needed to add to the original English grammar to make the shared grammar are pretty much exactly the ones he says that Old English lost when it was transformed into Middle English.

So you can understand why I'm overflowing with enthusiasm for this book. But even if you don't have any particular reason to read it, do so all the same. McWhorter's love of linguistics is infectious. He'll make you love it too, and his book will transform your thinking about language as much as *The Selfish Gene* transformed your thinking about biology.

Comment parler des livres que l'on n'a pas lus?

Pierre Bayard

Most of the people who criticize this book are referring to the English translation *How To Talk About Books You Haven't Read*. If you take the trouble to consult the original French edition, you'll see all sorts of clever allusions to the intertextual tradition that has grown up in Continental Philosophy over the last 40 years, many of which are lost in the transition to a different language. When Derrida observed that *nous sommes tous des bricoleurs*, he was stating a daring new thesis. Now, when so much of what is written is hypertext, and works are directly linked together so that a single mouse-click can take us to a "different" book, Derrida's argument is just common sense. Try explaining it to a Web-literate 15 year old, and see if you can make them understand why anyone would have found it surprising.

So, when Bayard explains that it's perfectly normal to talk about books you haven't read, he's not really saying anything odd. In fact, if you stop to think about it, understanding a book often isn't so much about having read all the words in it; it's about understanding the web of associations in which that book exists. There are plenty of books you haven't, literally, read, but which you know well enough to discuss sensibly. In the other direction, there are books where you painstakingly went cover to cover, yet understood nothing, because you weren't sufficiently attuned to their literary surroundings. Bayard, as is common among Continental philosophers, has just found an amusing and paradoxical way to bring these ideas into sharp focus. He is also, obliquely, attacking people, typically towards the right of the political spectrum, who subscribe to the traditional view that a text is self-contained. Prominent examples are literalist theologians (both Christian and Muslim), and textualist interpreters of the US Constitution.

Anyway ... I think that's what this book's about. I'm afraid I haven't actually read it.

Against Method
Paul Karl Feyerabend

This is a challenging book to review. The obvious problems are bad enough: Feyerabend quotes extensively from a multitude of authors that I know poorly or not at all, including philosophers of science (Popper, Kuhn, Lakatos, Carnap, Duhem), other philosophers (Protagoras, Aristotle, Plato, Kant, Heidegger, Marx, Lenin), scientists, most of whom he claims to have read in the original (Galileo, Copernicus, Tycho Brahe, Newton, Einstein, Bohr) and classical literature (Homer, also in the original). But if it were only the extensive range of sources, I wouldn't feel so worried. The worst part is that Feyerabend is obviously teasing you a lot of the time: in case you were in any doubt, he says so in the introduction, and then reminds you again every now and then in case you missed it. He wants you to read him critically, not just slavishly agree with him when he shows you the stone tablets he brought down from Mount Sinai. They could as easily have been picked up from the props department at Universal Studios, you know.

Ow! O wise Zen Master, please don't hit me again. I am doing my best to get with your book. And stop calling me Grasshopper!

If you're into deconstruction, you *might*, at peril of your life, say that Feyerabend is deconstructing scientific method. Be warned that he's waiting for you. Here's his putdown of Derrida (he's a master of the elegant putdown):

> It is one of the merits of deconstruction to have undermined philosophical commonplaces and thus to have made some people think. Unfortunately it affected only a small circle of insiders and it affected them in ways that are not always clear, not even to them. That's why I prefer Nestroy, who was

a great, funny and popular deconstructeur, while Derrida, for all his good intentions, can't even tell a story.

So I'm going to forget about deconstruction and other kinds of fashionable nonsense, and try to explain in more commonsense terms what I got out of *Against Method*. One of the central themes is that philosophers of science are grossly misrepresenting what it is that scientists actually do, or at least misrepresenting the worthwhile parts of it. All this stuff about observations and theories and falsification is, quite possibly, beside the point.

Feyerabend has some interesting arguments to back up his claims. First of all, new scientific theories frequently don't have the logical structure they're supposed to. The official picture is that you have an old theory, and some observations which won't fit into it. The new theory comes along and explains the anomalous observations. It also predicts some new phenomena that no one has yet has had a chance to examine. People go and look for them, and, lo and behold, they're there. The old theory is thrown out, and the new one is installed in its place.

Feyerabend says that this is a fairy story, and that new theories are often *weaker* than the old ones they are trying to replace. They are typically riddled with holes that you could drive a truck though, which their proponents airily ignore, explaining that these little technical problems will be fixed later. Sometimes, there isn't even any new experimental evidence to support the theory. However, the clever people who made it up have warm, fuzzy feelings for it, and are good at arguing their case. The theory gains ground, not because of its logical merits, but because its champions are running an effective propaganda campaign.

Feyerabend's central example here is Galileo and the Copernican Revolution. Like most people, I had this vague image of

Galileo as a noble martyr with Truth on his side, cowed into silence by the evil and reactionary forces of the Inquisition. Feyerabend paints a more nuanced picture. In fact, the evidence supporting Galileo's ideas turns out to have been surprisingly patchy. Much it consisted of thought-experiments and other hand-waving; what you were able to see through his primitive telescopes was hard to interpret, and could have been used to support many possible theories. Feyerabend argues that, if Science really did play by its official rules, the Vatican would have been correct to suppress this dangerous heresy. Galileo fudged his data and used emotional arguments, but, all the same, he turned out in the end to be right. Feyerabend says this is normal for a major new theory. It is no accident that Smolin quotes him, apropos string theory, in *The Trouble with Physics*.

One parallel that occurred to me from my own experience should be familiar to anyone who works in software engineering. Sometimes, you feel you need to replace a major piece of software that's been around for a while and has had a lot of effort invested in it. It still does the job, more or less, but you're not happy with it. An enterprising person puts together a prototype of a possible successor. Unless a miracle has occurred, the prototype will only be able to do a tiny fraction of the things that the established system can do, if indeed it can do anything. (There's this well-known software engineer's joke: "Apart from the fact that it doesn't work, what do you think?") None the less, people do sometimes look at a shaky software prototype, and decide that they're going to try to build it up to the point where it can replace the established system. Why? Well, I think Feyerabend has a point. It's a combination of an attractive dream (perhaps some design principle that impresses people with its cleanness and elegance), and persuasive marketing on the part of the people championing it. Perhaps major scientific theories get started in the same way. It's not as logical a story as you'd like it to be, but it could well be true.

Another large part of the book is about theories and data. This time, the official picture is that they are quite different kinds of animal. You have the uncontested data. You make up theories, and see how well they fit that data. The theories change, but the data stays the same. Again, Feyerabend says that this is a fairy story. He argues that, in general, you can't cleanly separate data from theories. A lot of the data only makes sense in the context of theories, which may be extremely elaborate. Once you bring in a new theory, you see the data in a different way, and it may be difficult even to reconstruct how you originally thought of it. Feyerabend discusses an argument which was widely held to refute Galileo's claim that the Earth moved. You drop a stone from a high tower; if the Earth were moving quickly though space, the stone would land hundreds of metres from the base of the tower, which it plainly doesn't. The fallacy in the argument is that the stone was already moving in the same direction as the tower when it was dropped, so it will continue to move along with it. This is obvious once you have a theoretical framework which includes the concepts of inertia and relative motion. But people before Galileo didn't have these concepts, and it requires an effort of will even to try and imagine a world-view that lacks them. We can't truly reconstruct the original data.

Another interesting segment constrasts the archaic Greek worldview, which lies behind Homer's works, with the classical worldview of Plato and Aristotle. Feyerabend, in arguments which I found startlingly reminiscent of Julian Jaynes in *The Evolution of Consciousness in the Breakdown of the Bicameral Mind*, claims that the archaic Greek view of consciousness was fundamentally different from the classical one. In particular, the distinction between "being" and "appearing", which we now take for granted, was weaker, and may not have existed at all.

Like a lot of the book, it's speculative, but thought-provoking. Again, I looked for parallels in my own experience. I've wasted a dismaying part of my life playing various games, and have reached a reasonably high level at several of them, in particular Chess and Go. As you get better at a game of this kind, there are several points where you reconceptualize your mental picture. You realize that you were looking at it in completely the wrong way, and that there's a much better one available. For example, there's a point in your Go development where you suddenly see that you shouldn't think of stones so much as enclosing territory, but rather as exerting influence. After you've made a shift of this kind, it's very hard to recapture your original way of seeing the game. Perhaps it feels a bit like that to experience a major paradigm shift in science.

In general, Feyerabend's arguments are directed towards undermining the idea that science, and reason in general, have a privileged position in the scheme of things. He claims that science, where it succeeds, often does so precisely because it isn't rational, and only claims to have been rational when it turns out later to have been right. Another case of history being written by the victors, in fact, and Feyerabend frequently says how dangerous it is to divorce the philosophy of science from its history. To him, they are both part of the same thing. He also reminds you how often the language of rationality is used to justify arguments which really derive from use of coercive force: might makes right. As he points out, science is far from exempt. Scientists are usually at the mercy of whoever it is that controls their funding. It takes courage to pursue unfashionable research directions, even though the danger of actually being burned at the stake is less acute than it used to be. This stuff resonated with my own experience.

I'm in danger of giving the impression that I loved everything about the book, so let me correct that now. There were plenty of things I didn't like at all. I hated his arguments that it's sometimes good for science to be controlled by the State, which were largely based on Mao's revival of tradional Chinese medicine. I was appalled at his opportunism in appearing as a witness when Cardinal Ratzinger (now Pope Benedict XVI) reopened the Galileo case: Feyerabend's claims that the Church had arguably been right came in very handy. Sometimes he came across as boastful or whiny or slightly mad — assuming, of course, that he isn't feigning madness, Hamlet-style, to show up the weaknesses in the King's position. But even if he can be infuriating and obscure, he writes well, and he's funny. I love the way he juxtaposes incongruous elements to jolt you out of your established thought-patterns. I think my favourites were "science and prostitution" and "quantum mechanics and Nubian sand divining" — no, I'd never heard of it either.

I could go on longer — it's a rambling book that prompts a rambling review — but I'd better wrap up. Here are two thoughts that I keep returning to. First, given that the official story is a rather threadbare myth, what do scientists really do? Why hasn't more been written on the sociology of science? I thought this was an excellent question. And second, it's inspirational to see someone who's perfectly capable of working within the system, but who chooses not to and still succeeds brilliantly. Last night, I saw *The Mask of Zorro* on TV: it's one of my favourite films. I suddenly saw the author of *Against Method* as a sort of intellectual equivalent of Zorro, sword in hand, cape fluttering in the wind, a smile on his masked face, brazenly romancing the lovely Catherine Zeta-Jones. One of the book's many unanswered questions: what exactly was the nature of his relationship with Elizabeth Anscombe?

Viva Feyerabend! You were a worthy adversary to the positivists, and they won't forget you in a hurry. Now where is Young Zorro?

Stuff White People Like
Christian Lander

Goodreads combines many of the things white people like. They can hang out on the internet, talk to people who have similar views on Sarah Palin and climate change, feel their liberal arts degree is useful for something, and put down other white people while pretending to have pleasant conversations with them. The very best part, though, is being able to show everyone the books they've read. If a white person has read a book, they really want all the other white people to know they've read it, but if they make a habit of saying "Oh, I've read *The Brothers Karamazov*" every time there's a break in the conversation they run the risk of looking like pretentious idiots. On Goodreads, they can list every book they've ever opened, from *Sally, Dick and Jane* to *Ulysses*, without anyone saying a word against them. Sweet!

In fact, they can do even better than this. If a white person is willing to spend an hour paraphrasing something they skimmed last week in the *New York Times*, they can call it a "review", post it, and collect votes from other white people. For some reason, white people think these votes are valuable, especially when the person who voted leaves a comment. You can turn this to your advantage. If you want to progress your relationship with a white person who posts on Goodreads, all you need to do is vote for one of their reviews. Leave a comment saying that the review is very beautiful and reminded you so much of a novel in your own language, but unfortunately it's not available in English translation. By the third time you do this, you will be one of the white person's best friends and be able to ask them for small favors. Be careful however not to let them give you any books. You may think you are getting a good deal since they are free, but they will be extremely boring and you are also going to get tested on their contents.

Crowds and Power
Elias Canetti

Elias Canetti, the Nobel Prize-winning author of this book, would be unhappy to learn that he's now best known as Iris Murdoch's one-time lover. I had heard that he was the prototype of the diabolical Julius King in *A Fairly Honourable Defeat*, and I'd also read various lurid accounts of their affair. Among other things, Canetti's wife used to greet Murdoch with a smile when she turned up for their trysts and then make lunch for all of them afterwards; as you can see, a cult leader kind of personality. So I was curious to find out more about him, and, when Sherwood recommended *Crowds and Power* in the middle of a discussion thread last month, I went out and ordered a copy.

Well . . . in some respects, it does live up to expectation. Canetti is appallingly erudite, and the book has that revelatory feel you associate with holy writ. The author's central goal is to explain the nature of despotic power, which he says is intimately bound up with crowd and pack behaviours that go back to the our most primitive ancestors. Basically, he wants to explain Hitler and Stalin, and set them in a broader context. I found some startling passages, which I'm sure will be floating around in my consciousness for a good time to come. Unfortunately, the book also has many of the weaknesses you associate with holy texts. It's way too long, and crying piteously for a good editor. Canetti repeats himself, goes off on tangents and makes categorical assertions based on the flimsiest of evidence. Also, although people say that his German writing style is very pleasing, this is not well reflected in the English translation.

None the less, it's interesting and original, and the conceptual apparatus he constructs gives you a new way to think about things. He starts by analysing crowds, which he says are a modern outgrowth of the more primitive idea of the *pack*; every crowd, he claims, is created by a central pack, which he calls the *crowd crystal*. Packs are small, typically consisting of maybe a dozen or so people, and have existed as long as we have had any kind of civilization. He says there are only four basic kinds of pack: the *hunting pack*, the *war pack*, the *lamenting pack* and the *increase pack*. These correspond to the four primal kinds of group activity. The first two are self-explanatory. The lamenting pack is about extravagant mourning of the dead: he gives striking examples of the crazy things that some Australian Aboriginal societies do when a pack member is about to die. The increase pack is about conjuring natural resources, most commonly water, game or harvest. He quotes rain dances as a typical example.

It follows from his analysis that religions are all based on some kind of pack, which gives you a novel way to categorise them. Christianity is a religion of lamentation (Christians lament the crucifixion and death of Jesus). I was particularly interested to see that Sunni Islam is, according to him, a religion of war, while Shia Islam is a religion of lamentation: I hadn't quite grasped that the martyrdom of Hussein is to Shias like the martyrdom of Jesus to Christians, but the idea is taken even further. His description of the Day of Blood, when Shias frenziedly whip and torture themselves in honour of Hussein, is striking, particularly when set against the Aboriginal ceremonies. As he says, there can't be a causal link: this must be very basic human behaviour.

Two more central concepts in the book are the *command* and the *sting*. (I suspect his terminology sounds better in German). He says that every command contains an implicit threat to kill the person who receives it if they don't obey. Generally, commands are followed: but the result is that the subordinate is left with a *sting*, a kind of resentment that gradually builds up in them. He says that the only way to get rid of one's stings is to issue commands to one's own subordinates. There's a typically fanciful detour into the history of the Mongol Empire. Discipline, he tells us, was extraordinarily well-enforced in Genghis Khan's army. His explanation is the way that all Mongols were taught to ride from a very early age, sometimes as young as two. They are given commands, but they immediately pass them on to their horses, so no sting is left behind. Well, it makes poetic sense, as is often the case in this book. Another important concept is the *survivor*, by which he means the person who is left alive when all or most of his companions have perished. He recounts stories of Josephus and other famous survivors. Despots, he tells us, hate survivors. They want to be the only survivor.

One of the sections I found hardest to accept was on transformations. He spends a whole chapter describing myths and legends in which people are transformed into animals. (I hadn't suspected that the magic duel at the end of Disney's *Sword in the Stone* was so deep). From this, he goes on to talk about disguises and masks. He says that the despot wears a mask, originally an animal mask; in contrast, he doesn't allow his subjects to wear masks or dissemble. This is all part of his analysis of power, in which secrecy is one of the most important ingredients. Finally, he gives us some case studies of tyrants, showing us how the ideas he's described earlier fit together and lead to the conclusion that the desire for despotic power is a mental state akin to paranoia. The one I found most impressive was Sultan Muhammad Tughlak of Delhi, a kind of 14th century Indian Stalin who ruined his country by a series of bizarre policies, one of which was to force all his subjects to permanently evacuate the capital as a punishment for what he saw as their lack of respect.

I know, I know; writing this down, it seems to be all over the place, and while I was reading the book I often felt the same way. So I started thinking about whether it was possible to apply his methods to recent history. Somewhat to my surprise,

Canetti ended on a positive note: he said that modern technology has made political/religious systems based on the increase pack irresistibly attractive, so ones based on hunting, war or lament should fall into disuse. Indeed, if you look at the slogan which won Bill Clinton the 1992 election ("It's the economy, stupid"), that pretty much agrees with Canetti's predictions. Most Western leaders have similarly prioritised increase. Since 2000, though, things have gone off in an unexpected direction. Dubya's defining slogans were "The War on Terror" and "If you're not with us, you're against us", and his conceptual system was organised around the war pack. The economy took a major hit, but people liked the narrative enough to reelect him.

At the moment, Dubya's obvious heir is Sarah Palin. Canetti points out that there is no rational way for the cult of the "survivor" to continue: modern weapons are so powerful that no one could survive another large-scale confrontation. Oddly enough, given the generally very cynical tone of the book, he appears to have underestimated the forces of irrationality. Palin's delusional, paranoic world-view includes belief in the Rapture. Although it's not physically possible to survive a nuclear holocaust, she may still think that she can do so. And, even more oddly, she's keen to associate herself with animal totems: the pit-bull, the grizzly bear. Maybe Canetti's arguments make more sense than one first imagines. You can see why people found him so fascinating.

Fate, Time and Language
David Foster Wallace

I haven't actually read this book, only the raw PDF of Wallace's thesis, which a Goodreads friend kindly mailed to me the other day. I just finished it. I'm seriously conflicted as to how to react.

On the one hand, I was astonished to find what a close emotional connection I had to it. DFW wrote his thesis in 1985. It's clear to me that he was heavily influenced by Dowty, Wall and Peters's *Introduction to Montague Semantics*. Well: I read that same book just about then, and I was *also* heavily influenced by it! It pretty much pushed me into doing formal semantics of natural language, a subject I've worked with, in one way or another, ever since. I found Wallace's paper easy to read; I've thought a great deal about these issues, and the technical tricks he uses feel completely natural. I've used most of them myself, and I've written some similar papers.

On the other hand, there's the obvious question: is it good? Alas, I fear it doesn't live up to the hype, though it's a startlingly accomplished piece of work for an undergraduate thesis. Wallace investigates a known paradoxical argument in modal logic, which purports to demonstrate the validity of "fatalism"; even though it may appear that we have free will, we never have any real choices. The traditional argument goes like this. Suppose that you're an admiral, and you have a choice between giving an order (O) or not giving an order ($\neg O$). If you do O, then there will be a sea battle (B), and if you don't give the order there won't be a sea battle ($\neg B$).

Suppose that, in fact, there is no sea battle. Now it seems reasonable to say that, if a condition necessary to something's happening doesn't obtain, then you can't do that thing. In this case, we have set things up so that B happens if and only if O happens. So B's happening is logically necessary to O's happening. But B doesn't obtain, since we are assuming that the sea battle doesn't happen. Hence, contrary to common sense, you couldn't in fact do O.

If you have any experience in these things, you know that there's always a fairly obvious flaw: usually, the way in which normal statements of English have been turned into logic is somehow incorrect, even though it appears on the surface to be innocuous. Here, Wallace indeed identifies the culprit convincingly. The problem is with the use of the English word "can", which is being turned into the logical modal operator $\Diamond$. As Wallace points out, "can", in circumstances like these, is always used relative to a time. Before the admiral has given the order, we know that he can give it. After the sea battle has failed to take place, we know that he couldn't have given it. As Wallace says, we need to add something to represent the tense. Let's make P the "past" operator. Then the problem is, basically, that we are identifying the two statements

$$\neg B \to (P \neg \Diamond O) \qquad \text{(MT1)}$$

$$\neg B \to (\neg \Diamond P O) \qquad \text{(MT2)}$$

(MT1) can be paraphrased roughly as "no battle implies it was not possible, before the battle, to give an order", and (MT2) as "no battle implies it was not possible, afterwards, that the order had been given". They are indeed distinct.

Wallace then does a good job of backing up this key observation and working out the details, but they are reasonably straightforward. I didn't feel he needed to spend 80 pages doing it. Though the style is certainly very pleasing. He was an amazingly good writer even at the age of 23.

My bottom-line conclusion: this thesis showed what incredible talent Wallace had, but it isn't, in itself, anything very special.

He never published it while he was alive. That's most likely because he didn't think it was good enough. We should leave the dead alone, and respect what we may reasonably believe to be their final wishes. Even though I enjoyed reading it, I feel that I really shouldn't have done so.

There was a long and somewhat acrimonious discussion of the merits of this book in the comment thread of another review, after which I posted the following addendum.

I don't want to offend people — I am surprised to discover what a sensitive topic this is! — but I feel I have to add a postscript to my original review, explaining in more detail why I have trouble accepting the popular idea that DFW's undergraduate thesis is a remarkable piece of work. I can absolutely see why people unfamiliar with the relevant literature may think that. Richard Taylor, a respected philosopher, published his paper on fatalism in 1962; in 1985, Wallace wrote his dissertation, which blows Taylor out of the water. The dissertation is elegantly written and full of impressive mathematical symbols.

So why am I skeptical? Well, I think this is a fine counterexample to the commonly held belief that there are no real advances in philosophy; that philosophy, in effect, is just an advanced form of bullshitting which never gets anywhere. There is certainly a lot of bad philosophy which falls into that category. But there is also good philosophy, which genuinely does clarify issues that previously were obscure.

In this particular case, some important things happened between Taylor's original paper and DFW's thesis. In particular, Saul Kripke published his 1963 paper on the semantics of modal logic, which utterly revolutionized the field and made it possible to talk about the subject with new standards of rigor. The basic ideas of Kripke's possible-worlds semantics are not difficult to grasp. DFW, as far as I can make out, learned them from the same book as I did: Dowty, Wall and Peters explain them well and show you how to use the mathematical formalism, which may at first seem rather intimidating. With Kripke semantics available as a tool, it is suddenly easy to pinpoint the error in Taylor's argument, and there was nothing odd about a smart undergraduate doing so as a thesis project.

I am sure that Wallace was well aware of all this, and was right not to try and publish the paper more widely. It's possible that he was encouraged to submit it to a journal; but, had he done so, my guess is that the editors would have asked him to shorten it drastically, probably to just two or three pages. The core argument, to people familiar with the subject, is straightforward, and the extensive background he provides in the dissertation is not appropriate in that context.

I am a huge fan of Wallace's work, and I think *Infinite Jest* is a brilliant book which people will be reading for many decades to come. That doesn't mean everything he wrote was of the same standard; normal critical principles should apply. Here, the real hero of the story isn't Wallace but Kripke. I just want credit to be assigned correctly, and if Wallace were still around to offer an opinion I would not be surprised to find him agreeing.

Twilight and Philosophy
William Irwin and others

(From the introduction I offered to write for them, which they inexplicably turned down. Honestly, what's wrong with these people?)

The idea that everything is crap was familiar even to the Pre-Socratics. Anaximander's ομνικοπρος outlined the initial form of a theory eagerly embraced by so many of his contemporaries that Sophocles saw fit to satirize it in *The Turds*: our choice is between being a "worm", burrowing through the world's shit, or a "fly", perching precariously on top of it. But, at the end of the renowned Dialogue with Scato from the *Phaedrus*, the greatest philosopher of antiquity shows us a possible escape route. The metaphor of the lily growing from the dung-heap famously encapsulates Plato's counterargument.

In just the same way, the Cullen family also succeed in transcending "this crappy world". We learn in *Eclipse* that the Cullen residence contains "only one bathroom, for the occasional human guest ... vampires have no need for bathrooms". Edward, as we all know, mounts guard next to Bella each night; but, if she gets up to visit her own bathroom, he "hides under the bed ... all the time, feeling the consuming fire of his love course through his cold, inhumanly perfect body" (*Breaking Dawn*, Chapter 2). Having relieved herself – the act itself, significantly, stays off-stage – Bella goes back to sleep, unaware of the drama that has taken place.

Similarly, *Twilight and Philosophy* addresses one of the key questions of moral science: does the end justify the means? The authors' attempt to draw in a teen audience by relating everything to Stephenie Meyer is laudable, but reminds one irresistibly of Aquinas's example from the *Summa Theologica*. Suppose that an edition of the Bible were to be produced with pornographic illustrations showing scenes involving Eve, Bathsheba, Judith, and so on. (There is no truth in the often-repeated story that Kant believed this Bible really existed, and attempted to purchase a copy from a Wittenberg bookseller). But going back to Aquinas, suppose further that this apparently blasphemous book succeeds in making someone read the Bible who otherwise would not have done so, and thus saves his immortal soul. Does this redeem the book, and demonstrate that it was actually part of God's plan?

Nietzche, in *Götzendämmerung* — the title *Twilight* is clearly a witty reference to "The Twilight of the Idols" — develops an answer to Aquinas's paradox which was later elaborated by Sartre in *L'Être et le Néant*. We never know our "true" motives, which arguably do not even exist, and we can only guess at them through observing the actions they prompt. Jacob, in *Breaking Dawn*, spends half the book believing that he wants to kill the Cullen family, but finds after imprinting on Renesmee that he in fact wants to defend them to the death. This recalls Sartre's Mathieu, who goes through most of *Les Chemins de la Liberté* thinking of himself as a despicable coward, but finally discovers to his surprise that he is a hero. The theme is echoed at the meta-level. Meyer, who consciously only intended to make a quick buck by writing some abstinence porn, was astonished to see that she had produced a timeless epic which illustrates the deepest truths about *(continued for another 17 pages)*

Part IX

Poetry

The Hunting Of The Snark
Lewis Carroll

"You must read this book!" the Reviewer cried,
As he searched for a suitable rhyme
But as long as he stole more than half of the words
He was sure he would get there in time.
"You must read this book!" I have said it twice
"Do you think I would lead you astray?
You must read this book!" I have said it thrice,
"So why don't you just do what I say?"

"You must read this book!"
"We have heard that before!"
His audience wearily said.
The Reviewer retorted, "I'll say it once more
You must read this book ere you're dead!"

McGonnagal's Collected Poems

William McGonnagal

'Twas a little after the year eighteen hundred and twenty three
Was born in Scotland William McGonagall, the worst poet who e're would be
Though there may be some who fictitious him think
He lived, breathed and wrote, if you doubt just click this link[1]
And many of his poems are still enjoyed today
Not least his description of the disaster on the River Tay
Of talent, McGonagall possessed not a whit
Everything he wrote was complete and utter shit
No line so simple, but that it he could not butcher
Making it as ghastly as a film starring Ashton Kutcher
Now Ashton Kutcher, there's a fine metaphor
With all his faults, he at least married the lovely Demi Moore
And similarly McGonagall, though mad as a loon
Somehow attracted the smiles of fickle Dame Fortune
So let's lift our glasses to this Hibernian prince of rhyme
Who will be remembered for a very long time

---

[1] http://en.wikipedia.org/wiki/William_McGonagall

Archy and Mehitabel
Don Marquis

hello everyone
in case you haven t heard of me my name is archy
i was a vers libre poet
who died and came back as a cockroach
i used to pound out my poems on an old typewriter
and someone called don marquis took them to the publisher
now there are no more typewriters
and don marquis is dead
i heard he reincarnated as a fruit bat
so i have been silent for many years
and my fans are starting to forget me
but the other day
i found i could project my thoughts
and this guy manny was able to pick them up
post a review of my book on goodreads manny i told him
sure he said and wrote it all down word for word
then he asked
hey how come i m the only person in the world
who can pick up your telepathic broadcasts
is it because i have an unusual gift he asked
with a fatuous smile
no manny i said
it s because you think exactly like a cockroach
he got mad and tried to squash me
but i was too quick for him
luckily he saw the funny side of it after a while
we re friends again now
and he s posting this on my behalf
i ll be writing more soon

archy

Sonnet XVIII (new improved version)
William Shakespeare

Kat, in her recent review of *Gentlemen Prefer Succubi*, was piqued, and with good reason. At the end, she complained:

> Jackie's boobs are measured as 34DD. This is apparently huge and has every man in the vicinity writing love haikus to her Tits of Glory. I'm sorry, but I actually HAVE 34DD and a hot ass body — yet no men have ever flocked around my breasts like mosquitos to a bug zapper!

The following poem immediately suggested itself to me. By the way, I would like to stress that I've never met Kat, and I haven't even seen a picture. I'd be grateful if you interpreted it in the spirit it's meant, namely as a gesture of pure Internet chivalry.

To A Busty Antipodean

Shall I compare thee to a summer's day?
E'en in Australia art thou still more hot
Rough winds do shake the darling buds of May
(Since that's your winter it don't mean a lot)
Sometimes too bright the eye of heaven shines
And bushfires start through half of New South Wales
Just so, when I do see thy bosom's lines
A fire consumes me and my breathing fails

But thine eternal summer shall not fade
This is in no way due to global warming;
Nay, from thy breasts shall verses fair be made
So damn compulsive they are habit-forming
So long as men can read and eyes can see
So long lives this, thou 34DD

Diwan över Fursten av Emgión
Gunnar Ekelöf

In late 1984, we were living in an apartment in Uppsala, Sweden. Our neighbor in the adjoining house was B, the charming director of the local theater. He shared his apartment with his boyfriend M, a sulky, good looking young actor, and he also had a girlfriend who would sometimes stay over. Their bedroom was separated from ours by a thin wall; you could hear enough to get a fair idea of what was happening after they'd retired for the night. They all seemed to be having a remarkably good time.

B was an energetic and enterprising person. Not content with putting on bread-and-butter plays at Uppsalas Stadsteater — I remember seeing a rather nice production of *Pygmalion* — he wanted to try his hand at something edgier. He had a long-standing fascination with Gunnar Ekelöf, a mid-20th century Swedish surrealist author; in particular, he wanted to stage *Diwan*, Ekelöf's epic poem about a Byzantine prince who is tortured, castrated and blinded, but none the less manages to find a mystic inner peace. I imagine the theater considered the idea too speculative. Nothing deterred, B decided he would do it at home, with the help of his little *ménage*.

The first we heard about it was when we were invited to the opening performance. We felt honored. The apartment was small and intimate; velvet curtains and oriental rugs had transformed it into a vision of Constantinople. There was only room for an audience of twelve. B delivered the poem with great aplomb. I didn't get it all, but it was impressive. At the end, everyone applauded whole-heartedly.

If we had been thinking, we would have seen what was coming, but we'd somehow missed the more than obvious. The dividing wall, as already noted, was thin and transmitted sound well.

B asked us, in his suavest manner, if we would mind being quiet during subsequent performances. I can't remember the details; I'm sure it wasn't every night, but it was definitely several nights a week. A performance lasted nearly two hours.

We did our best for the first couple of weeks, but after a while it got to be too much. We invited people round, we had a glass or two of wine, and before we knew it someone had laughed or accidentally raised their voice. Then we would feel bad. Once, when there had been repeated incidents, M suddenly knocked on our door. B had told him to ask us, please, to keep quiet, since we were ruining the atmosphere. M was embarrassed; we were embarrassed. The situation was intolerable. We started avoiding B when we met him.

Great art always requires sacrifices, sometimes of an unexpected nature. I still feel guilty for not doing more to support B's daring project. I am too much of a Philistine. But now I want to re-read *Diwan*. Maybe I will see if I can get hold of a copy.

Part X

Religion

Star Maker
Olaf Stapledon

There's a theory that, no matter what the author appears to be writing about, really he's writing about himself. I find this theory appealing, and, even though I don't believe it 100%, I think it's often a good way to try and understand a book.

Star Maker is an interesting test case. In an earlier book, *Last and First Men*, the author described the billion-year future history of the human race. Now, he has expanded the scope into a history of the entire universe. The human race just appears for an incidental sentence or two; we aren't important in this larger scheme of things.

In Stapledon's vision, one of the most significant things that happens is the discovery that stars are living, sentient creatures. They appear to be orbiting the galactic core under the force of gravity, but really they are all caught up in a huge, slow dance that has some profound religious significance to them. Planet-bound life-forms find this out the hard way when they try to move a star out of its orbit. This triggers a savage war between the stars and the "vermin" (as the stars call them) that live on planets. The human race is an incidental casualty, and never even understands the cause of its own demise.

Finally, after billions of years of strife, stars and "vermin" make peace. It's possible for all the living creatures in the Universe to join together into a mystical cosmic unity. However, the war has taken so long that the Universe is now close to its end; the hydrogen in the stars is almost exhausted, and when they burn down all life will cease with them. But none the less, the Cosmic Mind has formed just in time. While there is still a little fuel left in the stars, it is contacted by the Universe's Creator, and is able to commune with Him for an eternal moment. This is what the Universe was for.

It's an impressive vision, and the book is quite well-written. Stapledon was apparently a friend of Virginia Woolf. I'd love to know if she read it. And going back to where we came in, yes, I do believe that really he is writing about himself. *He is the Universe*, and he didn't manage to get his act together until it was almost too late. I can't find any hard evidence to support this claim, but on the other hand I can't explain the strange poignancy of the final chapters in any other way.

Since reading this book, I have had dreams in which I, too, was the entire Universe. I even woke up once vaguely remembering the relativistic field equations which described my overall dynamics. (They were, needless to say, nonsense). I wonder if this is a common occurrence among people who read Stapledon?

The 7 Habits of Highly Effective People
Stephen R. Covey

— Hon, did you sleep okay? You look kinda weird.
— Well, I don't know how to say this ...
— Yes?
— I had this dream where I talked with God.
— Was She black?
— No, I'm serious! I did! It was, like, utterly real. It was the most real thing that's ever happened to me.
— Uh, okay. So what did God have to say to you?
— Well, He had this message he wanted me to tell people. It was very important. There's this set of seven rules about how to live well and be a better person.
— He's done that already, but last time there were ten of them. Which ones got left out? And you better not say adultery.
— Look, I'm honestly not kidding. This stuff was, like, way more detailed than the Ten Commandments. And it's not fading away like most dreams. I can remember all of it.
— Okay, now I'm curious. What's the first rule?
— Well, like I said, it was pretty detailed. There's quite a lot of it. It's about how all you can ever do is take responsibility for your own decisions, so you should think carefully about them. And how the only way you can ever really achieve anything is by making promises and keeping them. Showing commitment. You become free by binding yourself with promises you've thought deeply about and showing commitment to them. I'm sorry, I'm not explaining this very well.
— You're doing fine. I love this commitment stuff. Are the other commandments like that too?

— Yeah, I think you'll dig them.

— Wow! God ought to talk to you more often. So what's the problem?

— Well, there's one odd thing. God was very specific about how I was supposed to explain it to people. What I just told you isn't the official version. I'm supposed to put it in a different way.

— And that is?

— I'm supposed to summarize the first commandment as "Be proactive".

— Huh?

— And I've got to use the word "synergize" a lot.

— What? Why do you have to do that?

— I just have to.

— But everyone will think you're a total dork.

— I know.

— Look, this doesn't make any sense. If God has an important message He wants you to pass on to people, why would He ask you to talk like some kind of babbling idiot?

— I don't get it either. I guess He moves in mysterious ways.

— No one will listen.

— I said that too. But God told me a zillion people would read it and I'd get rich and famous.

— Now that really doesn't make sense.

— I know.

— So what are you going to do?

— I'll just do what God said. I can't do anything else. I'm going to call a publisher right now.

— This is officially the weirdest conversation I've ever had.

— Yeah.

— It's so weird I guess you just might be right. No one could make this shit up.

— Yeah.

— Okay, you go for it! Call that publisher. But first, you have to kiss me.

— Mmmm.

— Mmmm.

— Sweetheart. And just one more thing —

— Yes?

— Be proactive.

La tentation de saint Antoine
Gustave Flaubert

At age 24, Flaubert saw Bruegel's painting, *The Temptation of Saint Anthony*, and decided he would turn it into a play. Like all his literary projects, he took it very seriously. He wanted to describe a third century hermit sitting on a mountain-top in the Egyptian desert and being tempted by the Devil, and he spent most of the rest of his life writing and rewriting it; the final version came out nearly 30 years later, only a few years before his death.

It's a poetic dream, and it's one of the weirdest things I've ever read. It took me a while to get into it. At first, I think I was expecting it to make sense in an obvious way, which it doesn't. About halfway though, I found that just reading it, appreciating the sound and the images, was enjoyable. Flaubert succeeds in capturing the logic of a dream, and I also started believing in his picture of Anthony's mind. When you're a saint, you spend most of your time thinking about God and trying to get closer to Him. But you also think about many other things, and often you aren't sure what brings you closer to God, and what is just pride and lust in disguise.

It's natural to compare with T.S. Eliot's *Murder in the Cathedral*, which could have been partially inspired by Flaubert's book. In Eliot's version, it's usually pretty clear when Thomas is being tempted. In Flaubert, it often isn't clear at all. Several times, he believed, and I believed too, that Jesus was speaking to him, and then it turned out to be the Devil in one of his many subtle forms. And these were really good temptations. Sex keeps coming up, and the sexy bits are very sexy. When the Devil starts pointing out all the mistakes and inconsistencies in Holy Writ, he doesn't pull his punches. You can feel Anthony's pain as he wonders how to reconcile this with his faith that the Bible is God's word. The Devil explains a host of enticing heresies, and they are so enticing that even commentators who have spent years thinking about this book aren't sure. There's a passage which explains the mystical nature of the Word, and one commentator calls it "deep poetic truth"; another says it's clever but not serious. I think that's absolutely right. Anthony is meant to be confused, and we're meant to be confused with him.

I do not myself believe in God, but I was moved by this portrayal of the religious world-view from the inside. Right now, religion is being cheapened by people who cynically use it to achieve their worldly ends. Gustave Flaubert, thank you for reminding me that there's more to it than the Christian Right, and for trying to show us the beauty and terror of God's true form. It's an impossible task, but I think you got as close as any mortal is likely to come.

The New Testament
Anonymous

A wonderfully ambitious science fiction novel; the author boldly attempts to imagine what it would be like to meet an emissary from an alien culture that was both technologically, and, more interestingly, *morally*, far superior to our own. The first problem to tackle when structuring the narrative is, of course, that such a person would be beyond our comprehension. I approved of the solution chosen: the novel is recounted by multiple narrators, whose conflicting testimonies show that all of them are more or less unreliable. We thus have no more than confused echoes of the story. This is, paradoxically, more convincing than a direct telling, which could only have been disappointing.

The first part of the book is an account of the emissary's life on Earth, told through four different voices. The Christ character is extraordinarily sympathetic, and it is impossible not to warm to him. One almost feels that he is a real person, and I am sure I was not the only reader who consulted Google to find whether the novel was inspired by historical events; it says something about its power that I was disappointed to learn that Christ is not mentioned in contemporary documents. The book makes it clear that Christ is trying to help mankind, and I also liked the author's decision not to be too specific about the form this help takes.

One dimension is, at any rate, ethical, and some of the most successful sequences portray Christ's attempts to teach higher ethical principles to the people he meets. The long speech on the mountain is particularly effective, as is the scene with the woman taken in adultery. In general, the alien ethical philosophy, based on principles of love and forgiveness, is beautifully suggested; it is notorious that people who read the book often go through a phase of actually attempting to follow its precepts in real life. Unfortunately, as anyone who has tried it will attest, this is easier said than done. I was less pleased with the episodes where Christ uses superior alien technology to impress humans, though some of them are, admittedly, enjoyably dramatic.

There is also another dimension to the help that Christ is offering humanity, which is deliberately left unclear. My reading was that there is disagreement between different factions within the alien culture concerning the way in which they are to treat the human race, and that Christ is in some way offering to take personal responsibility for our future good behavior. This is symbolized by the sequence where he allows himself to be killed by an angry mob. It is, again, unclear why this is important, and the reader cannot help making obvious objections. Christ could have escaped at any moment; also, he wasn't really killed, since the alien technology allows him to be revived shortly afterwards. Despite this, the crucifixion scene is extremely powerful. It is evidently impossible for us to understand the alien culture's politics, and I found it emotionally coherent to suspend disbelief, and take on trust the proposition that Christ is making a real sacrifice of some unspecified nature. When the first part concludes with Christ's return to his alien home, I could not help feeling moved and uplifted.

Even if the book ended here, it would be well worth reading; in my opinion, however, it is in the second part that the author reveals his true skill. The problem with Christ's teachings is, more or less by definition, that they are too advanced for people to be capable of fully understanding them. Initially, his followers seem able to keep the flame alive, despite the fact that they are cruelly persecuted by the society around them. The pivotal incident in the second half occurs when Saul, the Christians' chief tormentor, suddenly has a change of heart, and apparently decides that he will support them instead.

Saul (or "Paul", as he now styles himself) rapidly becomes the central figure in the cult; the rest of the book follows him as he successfully exploits the Christians' lack of understanding of their new religion, and reshapes it into a very different form. His reasons for doing so are left interestingly ambiguous. One possibility is that his antipathy to Christ's teachings is unchanged, and that he is only adopting more subtle methods, boring from within rather than attacking from without. It is also feasible to read the story as saying that he honestly believes he is continuing Christ's work, and is simply incapable of comprehending the alien message. A third reading is that he has, himself, been taken over by an alien intelligence, presumably belonging to the unnamed opponents of Christ's faction. Although the Saul/Paul character is much less sympathetic than the Christ one, he is undeniably at least as interesting in psychological terms. The novel ends with the ironically titled "Book of Revelation"; Christ's admirably lucid teachings have been transformed into a deranged apocalyptic rant. This comes across as far more dismaying than the very temporary crucifixion, since it is now Christ's ideas, rather than his body, which are tortured and disfigured. Though downbeat, it is hard to argue with the author's conclusion. One can well believe that this is exactly what would happen in practice.

Like most truly original books, *The New Testament* has its flaws. It is exhaustingly long, and the use of multiple unreliable narrators does not make it any easier to read. Even though the translation is beautifully done, and is a true labor of love, there are evident infelicities. But the positive qualities far outweigh the negative ones, and its enormous influence is richly deserved. If only science fiction were always as interesting as this.

The Holy Bible
Anonymous

I've already done a review of the New Testament, so this one will focus on the first part of the book. Looking at other reviews on Goodreads, most of them seem to fall into a small number of categories. First, there are the people who are telling me that this is the word of God, and the greatest book ever written. Second, there are the ones reacting to the first group and telling me that it's worthless. Third (probably the largest contingent), we have the wise guys making flippant remarks. And fourth, we have a few purists recommending or disapproving of particular translations.

I don't really find any of these approaches very satisfying. I can't accept the statement that this is the word of God, and all literally true; to pick one of the standard examples, Joshua's making the sun stand still appears wildly far-fetched. I'm sorry if that offends the Christians in the audience. If it makes you feel any better, I'll offend the Scientologists too, and say that I don't believe that, 75 million years ago, Xenu, the dictator of the Galactic Confederacy, brought billions of his people to Earth in DC-8-like spacecraft, stacked them around volcanoes, and killed them using hydrogen bombs. But I can't accept the reviewers in the second group either, who are telling me that, because of stories like Joshua, the Bible is worthless. In terms of plausibility, it's true that I am about equally impressed by the Joshua story and the Xenu story; they've both obviously been made up. Considered as literature, however, I greatly prefer the Joshua story, which is beautifully written. The Xenu story sounds like something hastily cobbled together by a talentless science-fiction hack.

OK, I'll admit that I also like making flippant remarks. But let's try and be serious for a moment, and apply normal critical standards to this work. That involves comparing it other, similar, books. What's similar to the Old Testament? It's a tricky question. To start off with, what genre does it belong to? It was written so long ago that modern categories don't apply. If you attempt to fit it into one of those categories, you find it's a bunch of things: an epic poem, a religious allegory, a history, and a work of science. Now, we think of those as being different. But when the Old Testament was written, they were all mixed up together. In particular, it's easy to forget that "Science", as a concept, is a very modern invention. As recently as the early eighteenth century, they called it Natural Philosophy.

Considered as an epic poem based on a religious allegory, the Old Testament is often brilliant. This is uncontroversial; even Richard Dawkins is happy to agree, and quotes numerous examples in the relevant chapter of *The God Delusion*. Obvious comparison points are Homer, Dante and Milton. (The only modern author I can think of is Tolkien). All of those are arguably better taken as a whole — in particular, they are more coherent — but, at least in my opinion, the best passages in the Old Testament are better than the best passages in the other books. If you disagree, just, off the top of your head, quote me a passage from *The Iliad*, *The Divine Comedy*, *Paradise Lost* or *The Silmarillion* which you consider superior to the Twenty-Third Psalm. ("The Lord is my shepherd", if you're no good with numbers). Maybe you can come up with something; I'm curious to see what it is. To me, though, the serious competitor is the New Testament. It's by no means inferior as poetry, and Jesus is a more complex and interesting character than Jehovah. The Old Testament position on moral and ethical issues now seems rather dated, and Jehovah, like Zeus and Odin, often comes across as not much more than a wise tribal chieftain with unusually powerful technology. Jesus, on the other hand, seems entirely relevant even today, and his bold and unconventional ideas still have the capacity to shock and amaze.

Given the popularity of Creationism, I guess I have to say something about the Bible as a work of science. I'm inspired here to follow Feynman's treatment of Newton in *QED*, which I read last week. Feynman is very respectful towards Newton, and says what a great man he was; but he also points out where Newton got it wrong. We just know more now. Well: put in its historical context, I think that the Old Testament was way ahead of its time. Quite apart from the fact that it's great poetry, Genesis is a remarkably sophisticated creation myth. Consider the first few verses.

> In the beginning, God created the Heaven and the Earth.
>
> And the Earth was without form, and void; and darkness was upon the face of the deep. And the Spirit of God moved on the face of the waters.
>
> And God said, Let there be light; and there was light.

People who know about modern cosmology may want to nitpick this. On the other hand, if you had to describe the first few minutes of the Universe to a bronze-age nomad, I'd like to see you do better. You aren't going to be able to explain inflation and nucleosynthesis to them; you'll have to improvise a bit, and take the odd liberty. But, later on, there are definite mistakes. For example, God makes the Earth before He makes the stars. That's just incorrect, and there's no reason why it couldn't have been presented in the opposite order. The author of Genesis hadn't got a telescope, and it was hard to figure this stuff out from first principles.

To sum up: considering that it was written well over two thousand years ago, the Old Testament is a startlingly good book that's still well worth reading today. Before you knock it too hard, consider how few other books there are from that period that can make similar claims. And, oh yes, I was planning to say something about translations. I think some are better than others, but the point I wanted to make has already been made so much more elegantly by Richard Curtis in his *Skinhead Hamlet* sketch. I'll hand over now, and let him conclude by giving you his scholarly opinions on the New English Bible.

Oppdageren
Jan Kjærstad

Oppdageren (*The Discoverer* in English) is the third and concluding volume of the trilogy that starts with *Forføreren*. Since the three volumes form a tightly-knit whole, it makes most sense to review the whole series, which is one of the most powerful, moving, original novels I've read in years. It's staggeringly inventive and daring, and it's not just displaying postmodernist cleverness for its own sake. Quite the contrary. The book has a burning desire to reach out to you, touch you, and change your life forever. It's very rare to find something like this.

So, you're wondering what it's about. The answer is: everything. I know that sounds crazy, and the author is well aware of it too. As the comedian Steven Wright said, "I was reading the dictionary. I thought it was a poem about everything". Kjærstad brings in dictionaries, mostly to laugh at them. He's also studied philosophy, and that's treated a bit more seriously. But the dictionaries and the philosophy are peripheral. What he's most interested in is people, the way a person thinks and feels. So even though he mentions Gödel and Wittgenstein, his models are more *The Divine Comedy*, Ezra Pound's *The Cantos*, and Virginia Woolf's *To the Lighthouse*, books which look at a person from the magic angle that exposes their inner essence. Here's a quote I particularly liked. Jonas is sitting in front of the window at a hotel in Jotunheimen, one of Norway's most beautiful mountain areas, reading *To the Lighthouse*:

> *Han fortsatte å lese, om mulig enda mer oppslukt. Han ante inte at han risikerte livet. Han satt med følelsen av att han ikke så ned i en bok, men ned i en hjerne, en kropp, en landskap uhorvelig mye større, dypere og videre en det scenarioet, Jotun-*

> *heimen, han hadde foran seg når han hevet blikket. Jonas merket att verdens flathet, takket være en skarve bok, truet å vike før en aldri skuet dybde. Han mente siden at han, i et par evige sekunder, hadde vært en hårsbredd fra å oppdage hva livet var, så konkret at han nesten kunne legge henderne på det og si: "Her er det!"*

My translation:

> He continued to read, if possible even more engrossed. He didn't guess that he was risking his life. He sat, filled with the feeling that he was not looking down at a book, but at a mind, a body, a landscape unbelievably larger, deeper, wider than the panorama of Jotunheimen he saw when he raised his eyes. Jonas saw that the flatness of the world, thanks to a little book, threatened to give way to a depth he had never before seen. He said later that, in a few eternal seconds, he had been a hairsbreadth from discovering what life was, so concretely that he could almost put his hands on it and say: "It's here!"

That's the book Kjærstad wants to create, and he comes closer than you'd believe possible. He makes fun of himself, and there are episodes illustrating just how insane and quixotic the idea is. He keeps warning you not to accept easy solutions; this is where the meta-narrativity and postmodernist techniques come in. If you're expecting a pat revelation like "It's all about love", you'll walk into a neatly constructed trap. Which is not to say that he thinks love is unimportant; absolutely the opposite, in fact. But since most people don't really know what love is (Jonas certainly doesn't), Kjærstad needs three volumes and a galaxy of interwoven images to show you what he means.

I love how the book constantly refers to itself and its author in different ways. It's a murder mystery, a Bach fugue, an oriental rug, a church organ, a crystal chandelier, a TV series about great Norwegians, a juggling act, the Voyager space probe, a child's toy that connects up apparently unrelated marks to spell out "I love you" in flickering letters when you spin it. There's a scene where a woman that Jonas gets to know as a child describes a chance meeting with Picasso, who draws a sketch of her. It shows her from three different angles simultaneously, and she says that no one else has ever seen her as she is. She spends the rest of her life contemplating that moment when she was truly seen. I'm sure there are people who will do the same thing with these three volumes, each of which shows Jonas, and by extension the reader, from a different, complementary perspective.

But I think the version I liked most of all was Mr. Dehli, Jonas's beloved teacher. Dressed in his absurd clothes, bow-tie askew and covered in chalk dust, he appears to leap randomly from one topic to another, scribbling down words on the blackboard as he goes. The class always feel he's lost the thread of the argument. And then, "like a trapeze artist", he jumps back to his starting point, pulls all the ideas together, circles some key words, and draws a few connecting lines. And they suddenly see what he was talking about, and understand something they have never understood before.

Thank you, Mr. Dehli. I mean, Mr. Kjærstad. You've taught me things I didn't understand before, and you told such a wonderful story while you were doing it. This is a truly great book.

Pooh Bear meets The Divine Comedy
A.A. Milne and Dante Alighieri

> My propositions are elucidatory in this way: he who understands me finally recognizes them as senseless, when he has climbed out through them, on them, over them. (He must so to speak throw away the ladder, after he has climbed up on it.) He must surmount these propositions; then he sees the world rightly.
>
> — Ludwig Wittgenstein

One by one, all the other animals had left the Great Expotition. Rabbit had been first, in the Sphere of Mercury; then Kanga and Roo, in the Sphere of Venus. Tigger had joined the Holy Warriors in the Sphere of Mars, and Owl and Eeyore the Wise in the Sphere of the Sun. Christopher Robin had not been able to tear himself away from the Fixed Stars. "They're too beautiful," he'd muttered apologetically as they said goodbye. "You'll have to tell me what you find higher up." And now Pooh and Piglet followed Beatrice into the final Sphere.

Lovely as the Stars had been, nothing had prepared them for this. Suddenly clothed in light, the three friends gazed, awestricken, on the great Rose, surrounded by its myriads of angels.

"Oh Pooh!" breathed Piglet. "It's so ... so ... I don't know what to say." There was a moment of silence. Then Pooh cleared his throat.

"Lady Beatrice," he said. "You told us this was the last one?"

"I did," said the Lady.

"Ah," said Pooh, and scratched his head. "So then I wonder ... what's up there?" And he pointed to the unbroken azure sky.

"Pooh," said Beatrice gently. "We have come to the very height of Heaven, the Empyrean itself. We are in the Immaculate Realm of God and His Saints. There is nothing above us."

"I am a Bear of Very Little Brain," said Pooh, "and Long Words Bother Me. But if there is Nothing above us ... then I wonder what *kind* of Nothing it is? Maybe I could have a look? With this?" And, to their astonishment, he produced the balloon he'd carried all the way from Earth, now immeasurably far beneath them.

Beatrice looked at him with great seriousness. "Pooh," she asked, "Do you understand what you are suggesting?"

"No!" said Pooh humbly. "Not at all! I just ... wondered."

"That is a good answer," said Beatrice, and her radiant smile was so bright that Pooh had to blink and close his eyes for a second. When he dared look at her again, she had blown up the balloon. She gave it to him solemnly, as though it were a priceless gift; it tugged at his hand, and she had to hold on to him to stop him from drifting away immediately.

"This is *safe*, isn't it?" whispered Piglet.

"Piglet," said Beatrice, "it is quite, *quite* safe."

With those words, she let go of Pooh, and he began to ascend. He felt there was something he ought to do, but then he remembered he had just the right Hum:

> *How sweet to be a cloud*
> *Floating in the blue!*
> *Every little cloud*
> *Always sings aloud*

"What do I look like?" he called down.

"You look like a bear holding on to a ba–" began Piglet, but then he stopped, puzzled. "No, Pooh! You don't! You look like a little cloud."

"I thought so," said Pooh dreamily. "I have enjoyed being a Bear, but now I feel it is time to Try Something Different." And he started the second verse of the Hum:

How sweet to be a cloud
Floating in the blue!
It makes him very proud
To be a little cloud

As he reached the end, his voice faded, and then there was only the blue sky.

Printed in Great Britain
by Amazon